The Love Disaster Diaries

Christopher Cisneros

Contents

Chapter 1

The thing about boys in elementary school is that they aren't interested in girls. Which, for me, was incomprehensible.

I never had a Cootie Phase. I never thought boys were gross, I didn't think they were stupid, and I definitely assumed everyone wanted to fall in love as badly as I did. This was before Benjamin Lancaster-the first boy who broke my heart.

And, that was my first lesson in love. Boys, unlike frogs, can reject you. You simply can't just catch one and force a kiss onto a sticky PB&J cheek. You just can't. Life hack.

Benjamin Lancaster was more than just a scrawny six year old in my eyes. No. He had potential to become my prince.

Not only was he the fastest runner in our first grade class, but he read at a middle school reading level and brought Reese's Peanut Butter Cups for snack break, which he would share with the day's line leader if they promised to call on him first. As far as I could tell, this kid was going far in life, and I wanted to be a part of it.

Being fresh out of my Kissing Frogs Phase, I had no idea how I was supposed to interact with a real life human boy that might be the one. So, I did what anyone would do.

I kissed him.

In Miss Rick's class, line leaders were chosen alphabetically by last name, and you got to lead the line for an entire week. And for that week, you were top dog. Not only did you have the honor of being first in the lunch line, you also got to choose who followed you. It was a coveted position.

Usually best friends chose each other, but for reasons I couldn't understand I didn't really have a best friend, then. But that wasn't a problem because I was hoping Benjamin would try to bribe his way to the top, and therefore, bring us closer together.

So Monday morning when my line leader duty began, I came to school with butterflies tickling my insides and sparks of excitement causing me to bounce with each step. This was the week I would finally claim my prince charming.

When snack break came, I knew I had to make my move.

Our classroom was divided into six tables, each with four chairs. We were assigned seats, and unfortunately, I did not share a table with Benjamin. No. I shared a table with two girls who made best friends instantly, and one boy who sunk low in his seat and never spoke. They showed no interest in me, and I felt the same about them.

I longed to sit at an exciting table with exciting people. I longed to sit with Benjamin, whose laugh you could hear across the room during snack break, and whose attention I desired more than anything in the world.

Fortunately, although our seats were assigned during class, we were allowed to mill about during snack break. And, that's when it happened.

The girls across from me giggled as they drew cats onto each other's folders and sipped chocolate milk from cartons--completely and entirely in a world of their own. The boy next to me sat silently eating slices of mozzarella cheese and reading a thin chapter book.

I sat patiently, waiting for my moment. I smoothed my wispy blonde hair, tried to look as though I was minding my own business, and desperately tried to stop my dangling legs from swinging nervously under the table.

And then...

"Hey, Hugo. Can I sit here for a second?"

It was the voice--his voice. Benjamin Lancaster's. And it was asking the boy beside me to trade spots with him.

My head swiveled to catch Hugo's fumbling. He looked up at Benjamin and blinked several times.

"Uh--uhm..."

Benjamin lifted up a package of Reese's Peanut Butter Cups to demonstrate why it was so important that Hugo traded spots. "You're sitting next to the line leader," he explained. My heart started to beat faster.

Hugo glanced over at me, and in that moment he must have seen the urgency that was written all over my face. He was the only thing standing between me, and a critical point in my relationship with Benjamin Lancaster.

Move, Hugo...Move, I ordered mentally. I felt my face flushing with the force of it.

"Oh, uhm, sorry," Hugo mumbled, eyes dropping from mine quickly. He scooped his things up and stood, eyes scanning the room for the least threatening available seat in the classroom.

I admit, I felt a little bad about that, but not bad enough to feel relief that he was shuffling away from our table and slowly sinking onto the corner of a chair surrounded by boisterous first graders creating milk bubbles.

I owed him one.

Benjamin dropped heavily into the chair beside mine and held the Reese's Peanut Butter Cups between us.

"Hey, Ingrid," he greeted me politely, lips spreading into a crooked grin--one that I instantly fell in love with. Curly blonde hair, freckles, crooked smile. Yes, he was the one. "If you pick me first, I will split my peanut butter cups with you every day this week," he bartered. But, there was no need for that. I was already sold.

"Okay," I said instantly, feeling my face warm in a way only a crush can manage to prompt.

But the moment clearly wasn't as magical for him, because instead of returning the heart-eyes that were practically leaping from my skull, he instead ripped the package open, handed me one of the candies, and walked off.

I guess he didn't get that he was the one, yet. So, I forgave him.

For the rest of the week things between Benjamin and I became routine. During snack break he would stop by to hand me a candy, and when we all lined up for lunch I would pick him first. Maybe the most annoying thing about it was no matter who I chose afterward would always receive much more of Benjamin's attention.

It was supposed to be me he was talking to in the lunch line. It was supposed to be me he joked around with at lunch, and it was supposed to be me he wanted to play with at recess. However, after he was picked first, he would completely ignore me.

All I ever got was a "Thanks, Ingrid."

I couldn't believe it. He was supposed to fall in love with me. That's how this was supposed to work.

But then something dawned on me.

It was Thursday night and Mom ordered pizza for the third time that week. That was happening more, and more. When my parents got a divorce and my dad moved out, suddenly my mom stopped doing things that she normally used to do--like make dinner or pull out the board games for Family Night. Now, we ordered a lot of takeout and watched even more cheesy romance movies.

And I was noticing a trend in those cheesy romance movies.

Some very important words had to be said before any real romance began.

Those words? I love you.

That was it, I figured it out. Of course things weren't going well with Benjamin. We hadn't said "I love you," yet. He didn't realize he was the one because I hadn't told him!

It was all coming together, now. I knew what needed to be done. If Benjamin still didn't understand who he was after being picked first tomorrow, I would make him understand. I would be the light in all of that darkness. I would be the wind in his sails.

So, Friday, when our routine continued as it had all week with no interactions other than candy and thanks, I decided to speak up.

During recess, after having endured another entire day of being ignored, I stopped him before he could walk out onto the playground for a game of Rock Man.

My hand tugged on his sweatshirt, pulling just hard enough to get his attention, but not aggressively enough to earn a recess detention.

He spun around, confused. I was a little nervous. I'd only seen this done in movies, and I felt a little tongue-tied, not sure how I was supposed to say what needed to be said--what he needed to know.

"What's up, Ingrid?" He asked quickly, tossing a glance over his shoulder at the other kids that had lined up for Rock Man. He flapped his arms impatiently, but it didn't even cross my mind that recess might be way more important to him.

I placed my hands on my hips, something my mom used to do when she explained things to my dad. "You've been ignoring me," I pointed out accusingly.

His face screwed up, and he took a step back. "What?"

"You've been ignoring me," I repeated, clicking my Mary Janes together. "I don't like it. You're supposed to pay atten-tion to me because I love you."

I was not prepared for what happened next.

"Gross!" He screeched, his entire body recoiling. "I don't like you," he told me, his words grating. "Nobody likes you."

The honesty of a six year old boy never hurt as bad as that did. It felt like the air had been squeezed out of my lungs, and my eyes instantly welled up.

No, that's not how this was supposed to go.

Anger surged through my body, an anger far too potent for a kid my size. "I love you and you're supposed to love me back!" I shouted angrily, my hands creating tiny fists. "That's how it works!"

I took a step toward him, but he dodged me. Now this, this is what I was used to--catching things. I was used to catching frogs and taking a chance at turning them into princes with a kiss. So, I did what I had to.

In one swift motion, I caught the front of his sweatshirt in my hands and puckered my lips. He pushed at me, and moved his head all about to deter what would come next, but my lips still found his sticky, PB&J cheek and planted a kiss there.

There was a moment, a split-second where my heart hammered in my chest and the hope danced across my mind, but when nothing happened--when instead I was pushed to the pebbly ground instead of embraced by the love of my life--I was crushed. Everything I ever thought about love was a lie.

This wasn't what the stories told me it would be, this wasn't the romance every movie portrayed, and six year old me was absolutely devastated.

What was love anyway?

The playground monitor rounded the corner, and I pushed myself off of the dusty ground. Frustrated, embarrassed tears leaked from my eyes as Benjamin ran off bellowing, "The Frog Girl kissed me, the Frog Girl kissed me!"

Tons of eyes turned to look at me and I couldn't find it within me to stare back at them bravely. Instead, I ducked my head when a couple of them laughed and joined in with the hysteria. "The Frog Girl kissed Ben! Ew! Cooties! You've got to wash it off! Don't touch me, don't touch me!"

Suddenly, I wanted to go home. I didn't want to be at recess. I didn't want anything to do with Benjamin Lancaster. I just wanted pizza and a cheesy romance movie.

Heavy with shame, I couldn't bear to join the other kids on the playground. I didn't want the other kids to scream and run when I got close to them. Not knowing what to do, I slowly made my way over to rickety, wooden bench that stood at the edge of the rocky playground.

That quiet boy that sat at my table, Hugo, was already sitting there. He always sat there at recess. He never joined in playing with anyone, he simply sat on the sidelines and watched everybody else. People thought he was pretty weird, too.

He looked up at me past his long, black hair when I hovered close. I wasn't sure if he wanted company. I wasn't sure if I wanted company right now, either--especially not the company of any boy.

"Can I sit?" I asked glumly, fists clenched, ready for more rejection. My eyes still stung, and I could feel the tears drying on my cheeks.

He shrugged, but I wasn't looking for a solid answer anyway and sunk down beside him. We sat there for a while, not saying anything, not making eye contact, just looking out at all the kids poking fun at one another and giggling when they dared to peek at me.

"At least you're not scared of them," he mumbled softly. I jumped at the interruption and he sent me side-glance.

"What?" I asked, puzzled.

"You're not scared of them," he repeated softly, his shoulders slumping.

He was wrong. If I wasn't scared of my peers before, I definitely was now. I stopped kissing frogs so this wouldn't happen--yet here I was. I just wanted someone.

I shook my head, frowning as I watched kids jump from one piece of equipment to the next as silently as they could.

"They're scared of me," I told him.

He didn't really seem to be listening. Another couple minutes passed without us saying anything. A chilly autumn breeze rolled through, and I began to wonder how much of recess was left.

Then, out of nowhere, he spoke again, and he did so in a bolder voice that obviously took a lot of courage. "They're scared because you're different. That's what my mom says."

He nodded to himself, and I crossed my arms.

"Are you scared of me?" I asked pressingly. He sure did take a lot of time mustering the courage to say what he did, and I was about to be offended if he was scared.

He looked at me straight on for the first time and shook his head. Relieved, I smiled a little, and he smiled back.

"I like you," I decided. "Wanna be friends?"

I was in desperate need of one, and I would take any opportunity I got.

"Okay," he said, the tips of his ears glowing.

When the bell rang, we walked in together. My insides were fuzzy, and my confidence redeemed. I may not have found a prince, but at least I had a friend.

I mean, somebody had to hold me back from getting into anymore shenanigans.

Chapter 2

Hugo and I may not have hit it off in the beginning, but after the Benjamin Lancaster incident, we became partners in crime--well, not really. I was usually the one getting into trouble and he would tag along, cleaning up my mess as I went. That was the great thing about Hugo, he could Houdini his way out of any situation. He was a mastermind at slipping under the radar, tiptoeing around eggshells, and hiding evidence. Nobody ever suspected Hugo, which of course meant I got out of trouble too. We were practically the Bonnie and Clyde of our grade.

Well, if Bonnie and Clyde were known for stealing hearts--or at least attempting too.

The only problem was Hugo and I saw people in very different lights. Where I was optimistic, he insisted otherwise. So, the occasional tiff was known to happen.

Our first really bad one happened in the second grade because of Clayton Krueger.

About halfway through second grade, a new boy wearing bright white sneakers and a football jersey interrupted our cursive handwriting lesson.

There I was, mastering the art of the capital S when a very brisk knock caused my hand to jolt and my S to come out crooked. Scowling, I glanced up at Mrs. Fitzgerald and watched her calmly cross the room, her face wide with a grin.

Obviously, this interruption was a scheduled one.

Like me, my peers curiously peeked up from their practice sheets to see who was waiting behind the door. Occasionally, parents stopped by to drop off snow pants or cold lunches that were accidentally left at home. Once, the principle came to drag Danny Ferris off for a good scolding on why you can't push people on the playground--a scolding Benjamin Lancaster never got.

But, what actually waited for us on the other side of that door was not a parent or a principle. It was a brand new student.

A brand new student who didn't know about my past of frog kissing or of my romantic pursuits since Benjamin Lancaster (all of them giant flops, to say the least. Turns out, kids don't exactly forgive and forget).

Hugo turned in his seat and caught my eye, his brows raised. I sent him a giant, gap-tooth grin. He knew precisely what I was thinking.

Clayton was not shy. The minute he saw that our attention was on him, he smiled largely and waved.

"Class, remember when I told you there would be a surprise at the end of this week?" Mrs. Fitzgerald asked, her usually scratchy voice high and excited.

We all exchanged glances with each other, trying to remember. No, she had not told us that.

"Well, here he is!" She motioned for Clayton to come inside and waved his escort, the school secretary, away with a short "thank you".

"I'm Clayton," Clayton told us boldly, making eye contact with as many of us as he could.

I liked him already. He was confident, and that excited me.

"Yes, this is Clayton," Mrs. Fitzgerald agreed. "Clayton Krueger. He just moved here from California, so I want you all to give him a big Michigan welcome."

None of us made a sound, we just stared at this new breed of person we'd never seen before: Californian. How foreign. How exotic. He was cool by default. He was popular without even trying. He was a Hollywood celebrity and I was seeing stars.

Unfortunately, Clayton's desk was across the room, so I could only see his profile if I leaned forward in my chair and looked past the rows of desks between us. He was untouchable...for now.

"I love him," I announced dreamily Saturday afternoon as I doodled hearts around Clayton's name in my Possible Princes journal.

Hugo and I sat side-by-side behind the low coffee table in my living room. Scooby Doo played at a low volume on the TV and a bowl of popcorn separated our work spaces. I could hear the whirring of the treadmill from Mom's office, so I knew this conversation was just between Hugo and I--secret best friend stuff.

Hugo's nose wrinkled and he stopped his scribbling to reprimand me. "Love is for grownups, Ingrid," he told me for the nth time. "You haven't even talked to him."

I rolled my eyes. "I don't have to talk to him, Hugo. I just know."

He leaned back against the couch to look at my journal. I had drawn my interpretation of Clayton's face and labeled the portrait with his name in my best cursive handwriting, giant pink hearts filling the white space. That's what I did in my Possible Princes journal. I started it after Benjamin, and filled each blank page with a new crush--all of the potential bachelors. When things didn't work out, I'd deface their portrait with a giant red X.

"You aren't the only girl who likes him," Hugo told me.

For whatever reason, second grade was the year that cooties became less scary, and I wasn't the only girl trying to steal kisses. It made me less of a freak, but also really irritated me. I felt like the hipster in all of this--I did it before it was cool. Nobody was giving me any credit.

"You're right," I said stubbornly. "Because I don't like him. I love him."

Hugo scowled. "No you don't."

"Yes, I do."

"Love. Is. For. Grownups," Hugo repeated through gritted teeth.

I hated when he said that, because he said that about every boy I told him about. But, he just didn't understand. Any one of them could have been the one, but how was I supposed to know for sure if I didn't take a chance?

Sure, I learned some things from Benjamin Lancaster, but that didn't stop me from wanting to give everyone a full-hearted, honest try. I just couldn't give up on my dream. I couldn't let the one slip away. Mom let the one slip away and then I didn't see Dad anymore.

Hugo didn't understand sometimes. Hugo had two parents. He got to see someone live the dream every day. I didn't. I wanted it.

"I don't care," I told him, tossing the pink crayon aside and flipping my journal closed. I didn't want to talk about Clayton anymore, Hugo was ruining it.

Hugo sighed and uncrossed his legs. "It's just..."

He stopped and I turned to watch him fumble around for words. He didn't talk a lot, usually. Sometimes when he needed to say something big, he had to pause and find a way to turn his thoughts into sentences.

His dark eyes searched the air above my head for a moment, and then he finally looked at me. "Everyone likes him, and when people are well-liked they can get away with things nobody else can. That's what Maria told me about popular kids."

Maria was his older sister. She was six years older than him, and a polar opposite. Where Hugo was quiet and reserved, Maria was loud and exciting. Hugo had me, and Maria had an abundance of friends at her fingertips. But, like Hugo, Maria understood people. And, when Hugo couldn't convince me, Maria could.

"Like what kind of things?" I asked, curiously. Well, if Maria said so.

Hugo shrugged. "Wait and see."

But I was already blinded with love. And, that's the problem with love. All you see are the good things, so the bad things seem okay.

Spoiler alert...they're not.

As the weeks went on, I fell harder and harder for Clayton Krueger. He cracked jokes during lesson, knew how to multiply, and had me entirely convinced that his dad was an ex-movie star. In my world, he was a total stud.

We didn't talk, really. He was the most popular kid in Mrs. Fitzgerald's class, and he knew it. Admirers swarmed him, and he basked in it. Nobody saw me as a threat, so my frog kissing past thankfully never reached his ears.

Well, at first nobody saw me as a threat.

Somehow, I turned into a gofer of sorts for him--not that I was complaining. At that point, I would have jumped through hoops just to get him to notice I existed.

It all happened because I was slowly trying to get my class to change their mind about me. I did this by being extra about everything.

Extra nice, extra generous, extra helpful, extra, extra, extra.

Our classroom art projects always went to dry on the back counter in our classroom. So, when it was time for art class, everyone would swarm the back counter to collect their work. It was pure chaos.

Somebody's project always ended up ruined or misplaced because nobody could keep calm for five seconds.

We're truly lucky nobody got trampled.

Anyway, I sat at the very back of the classroom and, as a result, was always the first person at the counter. So, I started to scoop up as many as I could carry before being mobbed and then delivered whosever project I managed to grab directly to their desk.

People loved this. But, it was Clayton in particular who really took advantage of the whole thing. And, being completely twitterpated, I did whatever he asked. I collected art materials for him, picked up the football from the ball cage at recess for him, gave him my dessert during lunch...anything.

In return, he actually noticed me. He remembered my name, joked around with me, and even chose me as a partner for reading time.

Hugo was not impressed.

"He just uses you to get stuff," he told me bitterly during lunch one day. "Thanks for totally ditching me during reading time, by the way."

But, of course, Hugo was being Hugo. He couldn't see that this boy actually liked me, and that I could not waste this opportunity. Typical.

Finally, I got the courage to make my move--and not the move I tried on Benjamin Lancaster. No, I better educated myself on these procedures. I wasn't making that mistake twice.

After traveling down to the library for reading time, I chose Clayton to be my partner and he agreed. I tried not to notice the hurt face Hugo made when I left him to fend for himself. I felt bad, okay? But, we're talking about the one, here. And, I was about to make my move. He had to forgive me.

Clayton and I called dibs on the highest level of the tree-house--a corner in the library with multiple enclosed landings and giant, blocky stairs. I stacked the pillows just how I liked and curled up right next to him--not touching, but close enough. He smelled like detergent and Elmer's glue from art class, and his yellow jersey complemented his brown curls and tan skin in such a way that just looking at him made my hands sweat.

We took turns reading out loud for a while, but unlike Hugo, Clayton was easily distracted and we never finished the readings like we should. So, in the short lull that followed an outrageous story about his ex-movie star dad accidentally getting shot during filming, I asked him the question.

"Soooo," I began, looking at my outstretched legs, my toes tapping together nervously. "I have a question."

He sat up excitedly, eyes narrowing like he was going to try and guess what would come out of my mouth next.

"If you're going to ask if I ever got to be in a movie with my dad, the answer is yes. Very briefly, in the background, you probably wouldn't even recognize me," he blabbered, his smile almost too big.

I didn't have a whole lot of experience in asking this question--my other romantic endeavors never got this far. So, I was forward.

I shook my head. "I wasn't going to ask that," I told him, and his smile shrunk, but that didn't matter to me. "I was going to ask if you wanted to be boyfriend, girlfriend."

He frowned, looking only mildly disappointed that I hadn't asked him more questions about his exciting California adventures. "Boyfriend, girlfriend?"

"Yeah, boyfriend and girlfriend," I confirmed, blushing and trying not to stammer. "You know. People who hold hands, and kiss, and write love-letters....Like the movies."

The word "movies" made him perk up instantly, and he scrunched up his face to consider my offer. "Hmmm...I think that would be alright."

I swear my heart stopped. It was happening. Eight year old me could hear wedding bells in the distance.

"Really?" I asked, my heart beating so fast I thought I might pass out from excitement.

I had a boyfriend.

"Yeah, why not," he replied, and stuck out his hand.

We shook on it, and that was that. For two whole weeks I would be his, and he would be mine...sort of.

Because Clayton was now my boyfriend, I began to do more than just fetch things for him. Sometimes I could get him to hold my hand when we walked down for lunch. I would swell up with pride when I noticed the other girls whispering and throwing dirty glances.

I was living for their jealousy. Yes, Ingrid Owens, the Frog Girl, was boyfriend, girlfriend with Clayton Krueger, class hottie. The attention and the status promotion had me on cloud nine. I truly believed life couldn't get any better. He was the king, I was the queen.

However, while I was practically walking on air, Hugo acted as though he was walking through sludge.

We hadn't really talked since the day Clayton and I became official. He still sat across from me at the lunch table, but he didn't say anything even when I attempted to start a conversation. He didn't turn to share inside jokes during class, and I stopped being his first choice for just about everything.

A couple days into my relationship with Clayton, I cornered Hugo on the playground and decided to interrogate him.

Throwing myself onto the bench next to him, I poked a finger into his arm. "What's wrong with you?"

He just shook his head.

"Hugo, I said I was sorry about reading time. You know I wanted to ask Clayton to be my boyfriend," I reminded him with crossed arms.

When he didn't say anything, I grew frustrated and stood.

"Fine," I hissed.

As I was about to stomp off, Hugo's quiet voice muttered, "How does it feel to get ditched?"

I looked over my shoulder, face burning. He just stared back blankly.

I knew he was right to be angry, but I didn't want to admit it to myself. I was supposed to be meeting Clayton under the slide, and I didn't want to be upset when I got there. So, instead of standing there and arguing, I walked off, avoiding muddy puddles as I went.

As I came up to the giant blue side on the other side of the playground, I noticed Clayton was already waiting for me. He had a giant mischievous grin, and he kept looking over his shoulder for the playground monitor.

"Hi," I said, as I approached him.

"Hey," he replied, and shuffled over so I could fit. "So, I thought this would be a good place."

My eyebrows pinched together in puzzlement. I looked around us, flinching when someone stomped on the jungle gym overhead. "What do you mean?"

Without warning, he leaned forward and quickly pressed his lips to mine. It was so light, I thought I missed it, but one thing was certain. Clayton Krueger kissed me.

I didn't have to catch him. I didn't have to hold him down. I didn't have to fight him for it.

He kissed me.

And, it felt weird. Not at all like I was expecting. Not like the movies showed. It was so fast I wasn't really even sure if it had happened. But, it must have because his cheeks were red and my heart was racing--and it felt like we were doing something we weren't supposed to, like we were breaking some kind of elementary school playground rule.

It felt dangerous, I loved it, and my face split into a grin.

"You said boyfriends and girlfriends do that," he explained, as the blush spread down his neck.

I giggled and covered my mouth with my hands. My first kiss was with the most popular second grader at my elementary school. I wanted to scream it to the world.

It was perfect. My life was perfect.

Or, at least I thought so.

About a week after the kiss, Clayton started to act weird. Suddenly, he would rip his hand away when I reached out for him and avoided eye contact. He didn't want to meet me under the slide anymore, and refused to be my reading partner.

I went home and cried the first day. I didn't understand why.

Why was he avoiding me all of a sudden? What had I done? Was my kissing bad? Was he bored of me?

Things were going so good, I was certain we'd end up together. But, after that first day, I was hurt and confused.

Mom didn't know what to do. She really didn't know who Clayton was, and when I tried to explain that he was my boyfriend, she let out something that sounded like a laugh--which only made me cry harder.

So, we went out for ice cream--and that helped a little, I guess.

But, I wanted to know why. Why was my boyfriend suddenly disgusted with me?

The following school day was the same. Clayton avoided me in every way that he could. And when it got to be reading time and he picked Paisley White, leaving me to fend for myself. I could feel my eyes welling up, again.

That's when Hugo volunteered to be my partner. After ignoring me for what felt like forever, I was never more surprised or grateful for it.

We went off to hide in a corner between two towering bookshelves and sat down. But, Hugo didn't open our reading assignment. That never happened.

So, I looked to him expectantly, not really knowing what to say.

"Ingrid..."

"Thank you," I blurted before he began. "For picking me."

He shrugged. "I couldn't let you be alone, again. You don't do that to a friend."

Friend. I almost forgot that's what we were. Overwhelmed, I wrapped my arms around him in a hug and rested my cheek on his shoulder. He stiffened, but didn't push me away.

When I leaned back, he took a deep breath. "Ingrid, Brianna told Clayton you used to kiss frogs and then Benjamin made it worse by telling him about last year. Paisley kissed him to get the 'Frog Girl germs off' and now she's his girlfriend."

Wait, what? Paisley's his girlfriend?

"But, I'm his girlfriend," I nearly shouted to the entire library. Hugo slapped a hand over my mouth to muffle the noise.

Slowly, he began to shake his head. My eyes widened in horror, fully realizing what was going on. Frustrated tears began to well, my skin grew clammy, and I wanted nothing but to disappear.

It was all a huge joke. Everyone was laughing at me--waiting to humiliate me. I turned into a threat, I got too high-and-mighty. I crossed some invisible lines I didn't even know about, and my classmates made me pay for it.

I was on top of the world for a few days, but now I felt crushed by it. My chest hurt, and Hugo must have seen the light in my eyes flicker, because this time he reached over and gathered me in a hug.

I felt so numb I wasn't able to hug him back. But, my skin tingled and my insides turned fuzzy like they had the day we decided to be friends.

I wasn't alone.

But what if he hadn't wanted to be friends anymore? What if my stupid infatuation toward Clayton had ruined it all? What if I had to find this out all by myself and I had no one?

Just like that my arms found the strength, and I turned into Hugo's side and squeezed him tight.

Right then and there I promised I would never forget about Hugo just because I was in love with some stupid boy--some stupid boy who wasn't the one. He was far too valuable to lose.

And Clayton? Well, I didn't say anything to him. I didn't want everyone to attack me at once, poking fingers and pointing out exactly why things happened the way that they did. So, I let it go and quietly dumped him in my head and in my heart.

Oh, yeah, and a giant red X just wasn't enough for Clayton in my Possible Princes journal. Cheaters go directly in the trash.

Chapter 3

Hugo's last name was Guerra, and the Guerra household was, in fact, very Italian. Every time I came around, Mrs. Guerra had an entire spread out-as though I was an entire party of people and not one tiny kid. I was too polite to turn down the variety of cheeses, meats, and breads she urged me to eat.

I loved it, but Hugo was a constant voice in my ear repeating, "You don't have to take it. Really, you don't have to."

His cheeks blazed red, and he stiffened every time he his mom rounded the corner asking if I was hungry. He was embarrassed, and I didn't get it. He had the coolest family.

The Guerra's owned a bakery downtown called The Bread Basket, and he lived with his grandmother-but they called her Nonna-and she couldn't speak more than a dozen words of English. I liked his Nonna because she always gave me sweets to take home. Maria worked for their dad part-time after school, and Mr. Guerra was always saying how excited he was for Hugo to get old enough to help.

Hugo just swallowed hard and subtly shook his head. I would frown at him. I certainly couldn't wait to be old enough to help out.

Mr. Guerra promised stuff like that. "When you are Maria's age,' he'd say. "You can come work for me, too. Practically family, no?"

And it was true, by the time Hugo and I were eleven we were practically family. Mrs. Guerra made sure of that.

Mrs. Guerra absolutely could not stand the thought of my mother and me living alone- just the two of us. And how could she? They were a family of five. So, one afternoon as I was leaving, she stopped my mom on the doorstep and asked if we'd like to come to dinner the following evening. If it meant she didn't have to cook or order takeout, my mom was sold. So, we went to dinner.

It was a feast. If I thought Mrs. Guerra spoiled me during playdates, I obviously had no idea what she was truly capable of. Fresh bread from the bakery, pasta for an appetizer, some strange dish Nonna made that apparently contained lamb, and much, much more. My mom even had a glass of the wine at dinner-wine she brought as a thank you to the Guerra's. They filled her glass twice.

Hugo and I sat side-by-side on a bench seat. His family was loud and rambunctious at the dinner table, you couldn't even hear your own thoughts. My mom was laughing...hard-something I hadn't seen in a really long time, and my eyes were jumping from person to person, trying to follow a conversation where everyone was talking over one another. But, when I took a bite of Nonna's dish and glanced at Hugo to see if he was enjoying himself as much as everyone else, I found his shoulders hunched and his mouth pinched.

I elbowed him lightly. "What's wrong?"

He looked at me and grimaced-well, actually, his whole body did one giant cringe. "I'm sorry everyone is so...loud."

I found myself furrowing my brows in confusion. What did he mean?

I looked over at my mom who was taking a sip of wine, her lips turned up in a smile while Maria and Mrs. Guerra went back and forth about an accident that happened at the bakery. Nonna was saying something rapidly in Italian to Mr. Guerra-who rolled his eyes. "Sì, sì, sì..." He kept repeating, "Naturalmente."

Everyone was in high spirits...everyone but Hugo.

"Everyone is having a good time," I told Hugo. "Really."

He considered what I said and scanned the table, lips pursed. I mean, sure, things looked a little chaotic if you weren't paying attention-but if you listened, really listened, you heard laughing and passionate story-telling and compliments to the chef.

This time he nudged me. "Okay, I guess. I know they can be overwhelming, though."

I shook my head. "They're perfect."

That made him smile-a shy one, but a glimmer twinkled in his eyes.

And, well, after that, dinner with the Guerra family turned into a weekly thing. Hugo's home quickly turned into my second one. My mom and I would stay there for hours after dinner, and while the grown-ups cleaned up the kitchen, Hugo and I would slip away.

The great thing about Hugo's house is that I got to hang out in his bedroom. Mom never let Hugo and I hang out where she couldn't supervise, espeically the older we got. Hugo's parents, though, they let us go to Hugo's room if we left the door open. They knew we weren't getting up to anything we weren't supposed to, anyway.

Hugo's room was smaller than mine, but way more decorated. I had the odd poster here and there on my purple walls, but Hugo's bedroom ceiling was completely plastered in them. Movies, bands, cartoon characters, and popular celebrities gazed down at us as we walked in.

I did a running jump, and bounced across the mattress, careful not to bump my head on the wall. He gave me a look and made a point of calmly seating himself beside me.

"Guess what?" I began.

He fell back and stretched. "What?" he guessed, voice tight as he reached over his head, making his t-shirt ride up.

I crossed my legs and scooted forward.

"I made a MySpace account," I whispered so that if Maria walked past she wouldn't hear.

Hugo bolted up, eyes wide. "You what?"

In the fifth grade, MySpace was old news. It was on it's homestretch as far as popularity goes. Something called Facebook was slowly beginning to steal the spotlight. But for a class of Michigan fifth graders, MySpace would do.

It was the place to talk to people if you didn't have a cellphone-something I wouldn't get the privledge of having until I was in highschool. But, that was only half the fun. You got to create an online profile, post pictures, and meet people.

It broke every one of my mom's internet rules-which only made it more appealing.

"I know," I practically squeeled.

If we're being honest, my quest to find the one was at, yet, another stand-still. I was tired of elementary school-I had a reputation there. I would swoon over boys both younger and older than me, but somehow they knew to avoid the Frog Girl. I was sick of it, sick of waiting. I wanted someone now, and maybe I needed to expand my horizens. Maybe my true love was one of the internet variety.

Hugo's mouth hung open in disbelief. "Your mom let you make a profile?"

My face twisted and I rocked backward guiltily. "Well...not exactly," I admitted, stomach knotting. "I did it last night and then deleted the internet history."

"Ingrid," he cautioned, pushing his hair from his eyes. Hugo wasn't one for breaking rules. "You're going to get in trouble."

"I'm not doing anything bad!" I said, defensively. "I just want to talk to, you know, boys."

Hugo shook his head, and the more pleadingly I looked at him the harder he disagreed.

"Rule one of internet safety is not talking to strangers," he preached at me, turning his nose up like his mom always did when she playfully argued with his dad in the kitchen.

I knew I was breaking rules, but how could Hugo not see I was doing it for good reason?

"What am I supposed to do?" I asked him, crossly. "I want to find him, already, and nobody at school is giving me a chance."

Hugo's eyes flitted away from my gaze and he began to pick at his bedding. He decided not to argue with me.

"I don't know, Ingrid. It just seems a bit drastic," he told me instead, not looking up. "My mom says there are a lot of weirdos on that site."

I groaned. Nothing annoyed me more than hearing that. I swore, one day talking with strangers on the internet was going to be as normal as saying hello to someone on the street. There were weirdos everywhere, and I wasn't going to let that stop me. I had a dream that needed fulfilling.

"Trust me," I promised with an encouraging smile, "I'll be careful."

"It's not you I worry about," Hugo replied, softly. And then he changed the subject.

Keeping my MySpace account a secret was easy at first. The computer was in Mom's office, and I got to be on it for a whole hour while she was home. She didn't hover, really. She just occasionally asked what I was up to. Plus, she didn't know that I knew how to delete the internet history.

I kept my profile simple. My "About Me" stated nothing but my age, a vague mention of my interests, and a very forward statement: I made this account to find the love of my life.

You'd think my previous failures at love would have taught me to be less abrasive, but I don't think I had a subtle bone in my body.

I thought the boys would come to me. I thought I would be flooded with IM's and secret admirers before the end of the week. But when none of those things happened, my confidence crumbled. MySpace was devastatingly underwhelming. Plus, Hugo wasn't good at keeping my hopes up. His negativity was really sucking the fun right out of everything.

It just didn't meet my expectations. Why was my class so obsessed with it? Even if they weren't cool or "emo" like everyone else, at least their friends were talking to them. Like in real life, I just wasn't fitting in.

I was close, so close to deleting the account, heartbroken by another failed love attempt-but then I got the message.

Now, I had sent messages to Possible Princes before, but nobody ever replied. And, if they did, they immediately stopped talking to me when I got "clingy".

Never before had someone messaged me first. And certainly not like this:

Sk8er_Dood666

sup babe

I'm pretty sure I stopped breathing. I must have ascended into heaven right at that very moment because my senses were on overdrive: white light, angel choir-hell, my life even flashed before my eyes.

"Sup, babe." How romantic was that?

Nobody called me babe. Boys called me Frog Girl, for goodness sake.

I couldn't believe it. How was I supposed to reply to something so incredibly saucy?

I said the only thing I could remember how to type:

xXPrncssIngridXx

hi

Yes, I was that smooth.

As I awaited a response, I did a celebratory chair spin and tried really hard not to squeal so Mom wouldn't come barging in to ruin the beginning of a romantic cyber affair.

Despite that, though, I had an itch-a little tickle. I had to tell Hugo.

It would be the perfect, "I told you so." See, the love of my life was on the internet. And, from his icon-a black haired boy with purple fringe and pouty lips-I knew he was real. And with a line opener like "Sup, babe," there was no way he could be a creep.

Creeps just aren't romantic like that.

Sk8er_Dood666

i cud b the <3 of ur life

The love of my life? This boy whom I had spoken only one word to wanted to be mine? Was this real life? Was I dreaming?

How easy this was! My love life got a fresh start on My-Space. I should have done this sooner.

I was ready to jump in. This boy wanted to be the love of my life, and I was not one to waste opportunities-I simply didn't believe in it. But, first, I had to sort out the basics. I had to know who I was dating.

So, I asked him the obvious sorts of things.

What's your name? How old are you? Where do you live? (This was far too intimate of a moment for a/s/l, or age, sex, location type lingo that I had tried out before-I wasn't very good at that slap-dash meeting stuff). I also asked what his favorite candy was, and if he had pets, and the kind of movies he was interested in (had to keep those real life dating options open).

Sk8er_Dood666

Zak, 14, Lawrence MI. warheads, pitbull named Spike, hor-ror.

Zak was so confident and dangerous. Talking to him was exhilarating. Not only was he an older man, but he liked extreme things. He had to be so popular in school-and he chose me.

I was a goner. It was love at first type.

Wait until I told Hugo.

xXPrncssIngridXx

ur so dreamy

I replied, but I was still lost for words. My head was spin-ning, my heart was pounding, and my eyes were permanently fixed on his hypnotizing blue eyes and pouty smirk displayed in his profile picture.

Unfortunately, it was the only picture of him on his profile.

If I had time, I would ask to see more.

Sk8er_Dood666

i luv u so much

I started to giggle in an uncontrollable way, and I felt my skin tingle and warm. He was the one. He had to be. It was instant connection. He loved me already. I wanted to shout to the world that I had just met the love of my life-and I was about to when my mom poked her head in.

In a moment of panic, I frantically closed out of the site-leaving Zak hanging after he had just confessed his love for me. I felt my stomach drop. I may have just ruined every-thing.

Mom's eyebrows twitched together like they did when she thought she might have caught me in the act. "What are you up to?" She asked, pryingly.

Thankfully, I had Youtube open in another tab (you can never have too many backups). Face still burning, I tried to shrug nonchalantly and keep my composure cool.

"Just watching Fred," I told her.

My chest tightened as she sauntered in and rounded the desk to get a look at the screen. She found nothing but the Youtube homepage.

She hummed softly and took a step back. I was on edge, knowing I looked completely guilty. I was a terrible liar.

"Alright, then," she said. "Just came to tell you that your hour is up."

"Okay," I replied, cringing when the word came out an octave higher than I intended. "Just gonna log out."

And, just like that, she left. I let out a breath of air I didn't realize I was holding in and I hurriedly opened up Myspace again.

xXPrncssIngridXx

luv u 2. g2g. talk tmrrw?

Sk8er_Dood666

k. its a date.

I smiled and signed out. Before logging off of the computer, I deleted the internet history. Something told me that being grounded from the internet would be a huge downer on this relationship.

Nevertheless, I was still excited about my new boyfriend-whom I had a date with tomorrow, by the way-and

I couldn't wait to see Hugo's face when I told him he was wrong to be worried.

Zak was a great guy.

Chapter 4

"**Y**ou were wrong," I sang as I sunk down in the desk beside Hugo's the following morning.

Everyone was slowly filing into the classroom, dusting off snow and avoiding small puddles of melted water. Conversation buzzed in all corners of the room, and our teacher wrote the first lesson of the day on the board while we waited for the bell to sound.

Hugo sat up straighter and pursed his lips. "Doubt it."

I ignored his snarkiness and propped my chin in my hand dreamily. "I met him."

His eyes narrowed. "Him? Who's him?"

"The one," I replied with a soft grin and a light blush.

Hugo crossed his arms and looked at me expectantly, like I needed to explain myself. I was happy to oblige.

"Remember all those times you told me to delete My-Space?" I asked, smugly. "Remember how you said everyone was fake? Remember all the moaning and groaning-'Ingrid, you can't do this...Ingrid, you can't do that-'"

"Yeah, yeah," Hugo interrupted, the curiosity in his eyes quickly turning to un-amusement.

"You were wrong," I sang again, this time more pointedly. His expression remained unchanged. "Guess who has a boyfriend, now?"

At this, his eyes widened in alarm and he began to shake his head. "No, Ingrid. Bad idea."

I scowled at him and lightly slapped a hand on my desk. "Is not!"

"Do you even know who this guy is?" he asked, scowling right back. "He could be lying. People lie all the time on the internet! They use fake names, and fake pictures, and fake personalities!"

"His name is Zak and he has a purple streak in his hair and he's absolutely amazing," I told him, lifting my chin and crossing my arms stubbornly.

Hugo paused and just stared at me, mouth slightly unhinged. The bell rang and everyone shuffled over to take their seats, but Hugo didn't even blink.

"That's it? That's all you know?" he asked in a low voice that I almost missed among the other whispers. He looked like he wanted to shake me, but he was stuck in his seat leaning so far forward I thought he'd fall out.

I sighed heavily and fell back dramatically against my chair. "You just don't understand love, Hugo. If you were a good friend, you'd be happy for me."

He shook his head and was about to argue with me when Mr. Riesman hushed us for attendance. Since he couldn't say anything, he just sunk back and turned away from me, jaw clenching. He wasn't having any of it.

But, why? Why did Hugo have to be so argumentative all the time? Why couldn't we just agree that he was wrong and celebrate my new relationship status? Why couldn't he just be a normal friend?

Maybe it was a boy thing. Maybe I needed a girl friend. She would understand, jump up and down squealing with me while we talked about how cute Zak was. But, looking out at the nine other girls in my class, I immediately knew that I was fresh out of luck.

Nobody wants a friend who is the "boy crazy" Frog Girl.

One time I told Hannah who I had a crush on, because, despite the mean gossip, we were getting along. Big mistake. She went behind my back and told everyone. That boy didn't want anything to do with me, and his posse giggled and pointed whenever I looked in his direction.

Hugo was all I had.

Put out, I mirrored him and turned away, crossly. I had to find a way to prove to Hugo that what Zak and I had was real. Maybe I'd let him come over to watch Zak and I talk. That would make him see.

Hugo was a skeptic, after all. He always had to see to believe.

Later that week, after lots of begging, I got Hugo to agree to come meet Zak. Well, if meeting Zak meant quietly observing the conversation Zak and I were having without actually contributing to it. Zak wouldn't even know if he was there.

The only reason Hugo actually agreed to "get involved" was because he was "worried I was talking to a forty-year-old hairy man with no life," and "he wanted to prove it to me."

I had to roll my eyes at that. Zak and I had been couple for nearly a full week and things were great. Every night when I got home from school, we'd have a "date"-which basically meant that we both got online at four o'clock and sent messages back and forth for an hour.

We talked about everything-or at least I did. Zak was cool and mysterious and made me guess things about him. I found things out little by little by playing 20 Questions. He was so addicting to talk to that I started to push the limits of my computer time-which only annoyed my mom. She threatened to ground me a couple times, but then I'd offer to do the dishes after dinner and she'd forget all about it.

So, really, dating Zak was fun and easy. Every day I'd become more and more convinced that we were made for each other. After all, the more I got to know him, the more I found we had in common.

When Hugo came over, Mom let me on the computer for two hours instead of one so that we could share it. When I told Zak this, he said he didn't know if he could talk that long, but that he'd try-just for me. I felt so special.

When we got to my house that day, I dragged Hugo right to my Mom's office and pulled up an extra chair-one he helped me carry from the dining room. We still had about ten minutes to wait for Zak, so I showed Hugo my setup for never getting caught and pulled up both YouTube and an online game site.

"Doesn't she ever wonder why she can't hear the videos or the games?" Hugo asked as he propped his head up in his hand, a single eyebrow arched questioningly.

I put a finger to my lips, scowling. The door had to be left open and he was still talking as though this wasn't a stealth mission. It's like he wanted me to get caught, or something.

"She doesn't ever ask," I told him in a voice scarcely louder than a whisper.

He hummed and stretched his legs out underneath the desk. My feet just barely touched the floor in my mom's desk chair when it was raised all the way up, but if he were sitting where I was, he wouldn't have a problem. Hugo was tall, and that was the reason for the permanent hunch in his shoulders-he always tried to appear smaller.

Not this time, though. He was purposely stretching out. And he only did that when he was confident about something. He was confident he was going to prove me wrong.

Ignoring the subtle shift in his composure, I eyed the doorway to make sure Mom wasn't hovering and then I logged into MySpace.

Hugo scooted closer to better observe the screen while I checked to see if Zak was online. He was, so I sent him a message.

"Skater dude six, six, six," Hugo muttered incredulously. "Really, Ingrid. This is the guy-"

I groaned and pinched his arm, to which he yelped and swatted me away. "You're being judge-y," I warned. We'd had this conversation before. He wasn't allowed to be a Negative Nancy while I was talking to my boyfriend.

"You can't really blame me," he grumbled, rubbing his arm. "His username alone sounds like bad news."

I was about to argue with him, but Zak replied to my message and Hugo's eyes now fixated on the screen. So, I opened the message instead.

Sk8er_Dood666

hi babe. i missed u.

Hugo scrunched up his nose while I beamed.

xXPrncssIngridXx

missed u 2. hru?

"H. R. U?" Hugo asked, confused. "What does that mean?"

"It means 'how are you.'" I explained.

It wasn't until that moment that I realized he would be asking that a lot. Hugo didn't have a whole lot of text-talk experience. Like me, he didn't have a cellphone. Unlike me, he didn't chat online.

This was gonna be a long date.

"Oh," he said, unblinkingly. "Why not just say that, then?"

I nearly face-palmed. Granted, I learned a lot of text-lingo from Zak, but still. It was one more reminder why we weren't keeping up with the cool kids.

"You just can't," I told him.

Zak messaged back.

Sk8er_Dood666

gud. u?

Hugo's face wrinkled up the same way as before. I replied that I was good as well and that school was boring.

While we waited for Zak, Hugo leaned back from the screen and asked, "Where does he live, again?"

"In Lawrence," I said.

Hugo nodded. "Isn't that only, like, an hour away?

I shrugged. Yeah, sure, I knew Zak didn't live that far away. I didn't know what his point was, though. Neither of us could drive, and I wasn't going to tell Mom about Zak and MySpace just so that we could meet-because we wouldn't get to meet, I would get grounded.

"When he turns sixteen he'll come visit me," I told him. "He'll be able to drive, then."

"How old is he, now?" Hugo asked.

"Fourteen."

"That's two years from now," Hugo reminded me. "Two years of not knowing who you're talking to-if it even lasts."

"Stop," I ordered, forcing the doubt Hugo just planted in my mind to go away. He was just being negative, again. He saw that there wasn't anything immediately off about Zak to point out, so he started in with the distance. "Real love lasts, no matter what. I'll wait for him."

"Oh, come on..." Hugo started, but then Zak replied, giving me an excuse to hold up a hand to stop him while I opened the message.

Sk8er_Dood666

Srry ur hving a bad day babe. anythin i can do 2 make u fell better?

"Convince my friend you aren't a creep," I muttered under my breath in reply.

Out of the corner of my eye I saw Hugo roll his.

"I've got something," he said. "He could send a picture of himself. One that's different from his profile picture."

I was starting to regret letting Hugo come and observe my date with Zak.

"You were supposed to come and watch quietly," I reminded him.

Hugo sat up straighter and pointed at the screen. "There are no pictures of him except for this one. Aren't you curious?"

I was curious, but I didn't think Zak and I were at that point in our relationship, yet. I didn't want to go and ruin this great thing we had going just because Hugo didn't trust anybody.

I sniffed and placed my hands on the keyboard like had my reply already figured out. "Whatever, Hugo. I trust him."

"Aren't you trying to prove something to me," Hugo taunted.

I glanced at him. His eyes were challenging, but he sat back, relaxed, waiting for me to take the bait. I couldn't help it. I had to prove it.

"Fine," I snapped, and sent the request with an aggressive punch to Enter key. "Happy?"

Hugo grinned. "Happy."

Zak was quick to reply.

Sk8er_Dood666

this is the only pic I hve

"HA!" Hugo cheered and bounced in his seat. "I told you."

I pressed a finger to my lips again and jerked my head towards the door.

"Would you shush," I gritted out. My insides were doing somersaults, partly from the thought of my mom hearing our conversation, and partly because Hugo thought he had something on Zak. "That doesn't mean anything."

The victorious I Told You So smile on his face was infuriating.

"Looks pretty fishy to me," he replied proudly.

Cheeks burning, I turned back to Zak.

xXPrncssIngridXx

pls pls pls?????

Hugo laughed and I pinched him again, making his confident chuckle fizzle to a hiss.

"No pinching!" he barked, glowering.

"Ingrid!" I heard my mom yell from the living room. "Be nice to your guest or he's going home and you're going to bed!"

My whole face burned to a deep shade of red, and so did Hugo's. We sat in quiet, both embarrassed for having to be yelled at.

Thankfully, a new message from Zak popped up. I looked at Hugo, and he nodded toward the screen, quietly encouraging me to open it. I did.

Sk8er_Dood666

srry babe. no. no more pics j this 1.

Hugo bit his lip hard, trying not to laugh as he crossed his arms and leaned back in his chair with a satisfied smile. "See."

My stomach had dropped before when my mom yelled, but now an unsettling feeling was expanding in my chest. Zak had to send me a picture. He had to. Hugo couldn't be right. I wasn't talking to a forty-year-old hairy man with no life. I couldn't be. Zak didn't sound like a forty-year-old. He knew all the text-talk. He called me babe. He was romantic and mysterious.

No. Hugo was wrong.

xXPrncssIngridXx

ok then. luv u?

Hugo snorted. But Zak's reply came before I could send him a dirty look.

Sk8er_Dood666

<3 u. g2g now babe. ttyl

And, that was it. That was the end of our conversation. Our first hour wasn't even close to being over and he never logged off this early. Asking for more pictures made things weird. I'd have to wait a whole twenty-four hours just to see if he'd show up for our date tomorrow.

With a sullen expression, I closed out of MySpace and stared blankly at the game site I left open in the second tab. It was quiet for a little while. I contemplated what my next move would be with Zak. I'd have to apologize, of course. It was just a misunderstanding, this didn't mean Zak wasn't who he said he was.

I couldn't lose Zak. I couldn't lose the one boy who was actually interested in me, the boy who wanted to be the love of my life. He called me babe, he made me feel special. I felt like we had so much in common despite his dangerous interests and mysterious nature. He was so perfect. I wanted it to last forever.

Hugo was wrong about him.

After sitting like this for a couple minutes, Hugo reached out and placed a reassuring hand on mine, one that told me he was sorry. He saw how upset I was, and now he felt bad. I pulled my hand away.

He didn't take this seriously and now I didn't know if my boyfriend was still mine.

His hand lingered above mine for a moment, but then returned to his lap.

"Wanna do something else?" he offered hesitantly.

It was a good offer. I didn't want to think about Zak anymore today, but I didn't want to think about Hugo either-much less continue to hang out with him. But, his mom wasn't going to pick him up until six-thirty, so I had to agree.

We ended up leaving Mom's office to watch Avatar: The Last Airbender and play Sorry!-which, I proceeded to crush him in. Admittedly, that did make me feel better.

I continued to give him the cold shoulder, though. He deserved that.

That weekend, the unthinkable happened.

Saturday, I nervously waited for four o'clock to roll around. That's when my date with Zak always was. But, this time, I wasn't sure if that date was going to happen. I still felt so stupid about the conversation that took place yesterday, and even though I decided Hugo wasn't entirely to blame, I still couldn't help but feel like things with Zak would have gone great yesterday if I hadn't taken his advice.

I tried to keep myself busy. I finished all my homework, doodled in my Possible Princes journal, even cleaned my room. When four o'clock finally hit, I knocked on my mother's office door. She'd been in there for a while, and I didn't know if she was too busy to give me the computer for an hour or if I had to reschedule.

Part of me didn't care what the outcome would be.

My mother answered my knock saying, "Yes, Ingrid. Good timing, come on in."

I froze. There was something weird about her voice-something accusatory yet sugar sweet. My palms began to sweat. What had I done? I must have done something wrong. That was her "Aha! Caught you!" voice.

That's when it dawned on me. Yesterday when I logged off the computer, I forgot to delete the internet history. Suddenly, I didn't want to get into the office at all. Somehow I knew I'd never be talking to Zak ever again. Our relationship will have ended on an awkward note I'd never get to fix-just like every other failed relationship I ever had.

But I knew I had to go inside and face her. So, with shaky hands I opened the door, and with jelly legs I shuffled in. My head hung low. Guilty as charged, no need for a trial.

My mom looked up from the computer with a waiting expression and laser eyes. "Looks like you already know what's up," she said.

I was grounded for life.

Who cared about Zak? I was never seeing the light of day ever again.

I met her eyes but the shame was too much, and I immediately looked back down at my socked feet. You remember things like that when you're about to die. I remember wearing pink socks and wondering if the torture would ever end.

"I've just spent the last hour or so talking to this," she raised her hands to do air quotes. "Zak you've been chatting with."

Oh, no. I felt bile rising. That was so embarrassing. She had seen my chat history.

"There's a reason I said you were not allowed to make an account on this site," she scolded me, her voice suddenly lower, angrier. "So, first of all, you're grounded from all electronics until you've regained my trust."

Not even love could save me, now. So, I just nodded.

"Second of all," she continued. "I think you should know that Zak's real name is Violet."

The surprise was like whip lash. My head flew up, my eyes bulged from my head, my lungs forgot what they were supposed to do with air.

All I could do was cry out, "What?"

Yes, Zak's real name was Violet. I was talking to neither a fourteen-year-old boy nor a forty-year-old man, but to a twelve year old girl in Lawrence, Michigan who enjoyed trolling people on the internet. That boy in her profile picture is something you could get off a Google image search.

To sum it all up, while I was falling in love, she was falling out of her chair laughing.

When my mom found out I was talking to some stranger on the internet who vaguely answered my questions and didn't have more than one picture to offer, like Hugo she immediately thought it was some pervert trying to seduce me. So, she decided to confront this 'Zak,' saying that she was going to call the police and make sure he was never allowed on MySpace ever again. That's all Violet needed to hear before she folded, worried she'd get in trouble.

While I stood in stunned silence, my mother gave me the longest lecture on internet safety that has ever been and then blocked MySpace, Facebook and any other chat sites that came up when she searched Google.

So, we were all wrong about Sk8er_Dood666 in the end. Not that it made any difference to Hugo. Although he was relieved to hear Zak wasn't some creepy old guy messaging me from his mother's basement, he found it only one hundred times more amusing that I'd been catfished by a twelve year old girl. He laughed so hard Maria had to loan him her inhaler.

And that concludes the internet dating portion of my life. Never again. Not after Violet.

It does make me wonder, though. If someone asks if I've ever been in a same-sex relationship, do I say yes?

Chapter 5

For some, middle school conjures up memories of embarrassing hairdos, awkward growing periods, and cringe-worthy social media status updates. And, alright, I wasn't exempt from either of those things. I wore too many sparkly green bobby pins, started wearing bras, and-since I was still banned from every social media site known to man-said a lot of cringe-worthy things out loud. But middle school was also where things started to change for Hugo and I. It was a light at the end of the dark tunnel that was elementary school.

The beauty of middle school? It was a fresh start.

There was only one public middle school in the area, whereas there were three elementary schools. When the transition from elementary to middle school came, all three elementary schools dumped their pre-teen graduates into one pool and waited to see who would sink and who would surface.

I intended to surface, and I was dragging Hugo up with me.

No longer would we carry the stigma's our old peers forced upon us, we were free. We would be among other students who had no idea of our past. Hugo would no longer be the quiet kid who stuttered when called on and sat on the bench watching everyone else during recess. I would no longer be the boy crazy Frog Girl. We would be two regular kids, just like everyone else.

I couldn't wait for summer to be over. I couldn't wait for the new life that was waiting for me, and the new boys. The only boy I saw all summer was Hugo.

And, I mean, Hugo was just Hugo.

A new world of Possible Princes awaited me. I daydreamed about the ways we would meet. Our eyes might meet from across the room in slow motion, I might drop my book and he'd help pick them up, we could hate each other and then get assigned to work on a class project together and fall in love despite the odds.

I couldn't wait to find out.

And, even though I barely slept the night before my first day, I bounced out of my bed at the first sound of my alarm, straightened my hair and pinned it away from my face with my favorite sparkly green bobby pins, and waited for Mrs. Guerra to pick me up.

That was the other exciting thing. Now Hugo and I were carpooling to school.

My stomach gurgled, but I was so nervous I feared eating would make me sick. I had to take deep, calming breaths as I waited for the red minivan to roll down the street.

After what felt like eternity, the Guerra minivan stopped in front of my house. I bounded down the sidewalk and hopped into the backseat beside Hugo. I was all smiles and bouncing knees, but Hugo was white faced and doe-eyed.

"Someone looks excited," Mrs. Guerra commented, her eyes meeting mine in the rearview mirror with a quick wink.

I nodded enthusiastically and jostled Hugo's arm. "Aren't you excited?" I asked.

His mouth opened for a second and then snapped shut, his face twisting. "I think...I might throw up," he finally managed to say.

"Pshhh." Maria turned in the passenger's seat to look at us. "Middle school is easy. You'll be just fine."

I grinned, believing her instantly, and looked to Hugo. He just frowned.

"Easy for you to say," he shot back. "Everyone loves you."

She waved a hand and faced forward. "Whatever, Hugo. Be dramatic, but you've got Ingrid."

My smile only grew wider. Nothing boosted my confidence more than Maria's approval. She was going to be a junior in high school-a popular junior in high school. Her words meant everything to me. If she thought I could get us through the day, then I knew I could.

"Hear that," I said. "You've got me. I'll make sure our day is amazing."

He sent me a wary glance and seemed to hold his breath. I got it, he was incredibly tall, he'd stick out like a sore thumb and he hated the attention. But, we were on a mission to make new friends and find new Princes, and if I had to drag him by the hand I would.

The middle school was a giant brick building with multiple floors and a massive entrance. The drop-off area was backed up with cars all the way back to the street. Students wove through traffic with brand-new backpacks on their backs and excitement in their smiles. Groups gathered around the front door, friends hugging each other after the long break and recounting crazy summer stories. I was no fool, I knew the shininess would rust, but right then, in that moment, I was ready to explode from the car and join them.

But, while I unbuckled and prepared to book it, Hugo melted into the car seat with his hands clamped to the armrests.

Mrs. Guerra braked and looked back to see us off. I swung the van door open and jumped out.

"Thank you, Mrs. Guerra," I sang politely. She smiled, and then we both looked to Hugo.

"Off you go," she told him.

"You know," he said breathlessly. "I'm really not feeling all that great-hey!"

Maria had climbed between the seats and unbuckled his seatbelt. He gave her the dirtiest look he could muster.

"They can smell fear," she warned. His eyes grew.

"Come on, Hugo," I whined impatiently. "You're holding up traffic."

And, he was. A car behind Mrs. Guerra honked rather obnoxiously, and I clamped my hands over my ears.

Seeing he was only making a scene-something he usually went to great lengths to avoid-he reluctantly followed me. Mrs. Guerra managed to press a kiss to his cheek as he passed her, and red lipstick smudged against his skin.

"Have a great day!" She called out to us just as he yanked the door shut.

After she drove away, I rubbed the lipstick off his cheek and gripped his hand.

While I led us toward the front door, I squeezed his hand and reminded him, "Time for a second chance."

After being in a classroom of twenty kids, give or take a couple kids, I was not prepared for the chaos that was a middle school hallway. They were everywhere. Old faces, new faces, people that looked vaguely familiar-they were there. I tried desperately to drink it all in, but with Hugo attached to my hand, it was hard. He looked shell-shocked. His eyes were darting everywhere, I wasn't sure if he was breathing, and I could feel the pulse in his hand beating at a concerning speed.

Thankfully, when we picked up our schedules and realized we had the same homeroom, he took a breath of relief.

"Thank god," he muttered. "I didn't want to find that all by myself."

Not that it would have been much trouble, anyway. Each grade had their own floor. The eighth graders were on the third, the sixth graders had the first. Everything we needed was pretty much all in one hallway. That helped with the stress, too. Now, I could focus on the new people I was surrounded by.

Unfortunately, nobody really got to talk much all day. Except for icebreakers and short introductions, the teachers had the floor, and they used it to discuss class expectations and explain the curriculum.

I had four of my seven classes with Hugo, and so between passing time we decided to meet by his locker before heading down to lunch. That way, we wouldn't be alone.

The cafeteria was way bigger than the one we had in elementary school. And the tables were different too. We used to have one long table for our entire grade to sit at, but here multiple small tables that could seat about six filled the room. Before getting in line for food, kids were claiming tables with hoodies and lunch boxes.

Following their lead, Hugo and I found an empty table and did the same, leaving my pink sweater draped over the shiny gray surface. However, when we returned with our food, we found a few people sitting at the table we claimed.

"Sorry," a girl with curly red hair said as we approached. "Hope you don't mind. There weren't any empty tables when we got here."

Confused, I frowned down at the two people sitting there. Were they kicking us out? I was used to that kind of thing.

Hugo hesitated, but then set his tray across from hers.

"Um, sure that's okay, Josie," he told her in a soft voice as he sat down.

I paused, unable to do anything but blink. What?

I mean, I wasn't going to say no to an opportunity to make new friends, but...what? Since when did Hugo know a Josie? When did he have time to make friends?

Noticing that I wasn't sitting down beside him, Hugo looked back at me, jolting when he realized I was gazing at the scene in puzzlement.

"Oh-uh, Ingrid. This is Josie, and her...friend?" He guessed, and then shrugged. "We have civics together."

Josie smiled up at me with a shiny, metal smile. Nodding, I sat down across from a dark-skinned boy with a shaved head and pretty brown eyes. Those eyes made my heart flutter, and I could feel the blush burn my cheeks.

"It's Joslyn, actually," Josie informed me, pulling my attention back towards her. "But people call me Josie. Oh, and this is Micah."

Both Hugo and I nodded at the boy as he was introduced, and I couldn't help but smile my warmest smile. He was making my stomach do all sorts of gymnastics. He kept his eyes on Hugo while Josie talked, though.

"Like I said, sorry for just inviting ourselves over. I recognized your girlfriend's sweater and thought you wouldn't mind. You seemed nice in class," she explained further, spinning her water bottle between her hands.

Girlfriend...wait, did she say girlfriend?

My eyes unglued from Micah's face and my head jerked towards her, mouth agape. Hugo was struggling for words, too. Except his face turned blank and his ears started to change color. Our wide eyes were both on hers.

"Excuse me," I choked. "What?"

Josie looked between us, her smile faltering a little. "You guys are a couple right? You were holding hands this morning...I thought..."

Hugo and I both started shaking our heads in frantic unison. He started stuttering nonsense the way he did when he was asked a question he wasn't prepared for, and I laughed nervously, glancing at Micah.

That boy needed to know I was single.

"We're just friends," I assured him-them.

She looked from Hugo's blushing skin to my stiff posture and back. "You don't look so sure..."

At this, Micah laughed. My attention found him, again. He had a slightly silly laugh, and I lost my words, embarrassed that that laugh was directed at me-us.

Hugo coughed, answering in my momentary absence, "We're not not sure, just together-not together, I mean....N ot...together."

Both Josie and Micah were laughing, now, and I wanted to fade into the walls, melt to the floors, disappear into the void.

I smacked a hand over my face, and slowly lowered my forehead to the table. Hugo's entire face was so red I thought he was going to burst into tears.

"Aw, how cute." Josie giggled, pointing at Hugo's flushed face. "You totally like her, then."

No. NO.

I sat straight up and shook my head furiously enough to make up for the fact that Hugo was frozen.

"Sorry, nope," I told her, a bit of frustration edging into my voice. This was going to end, and it was going to end, now. "Hugo doesn't have a crush on me, he doesn't have crushes on any girl. He's shy and you're embarrassing him."

Josie blinked a couple times in stunned silence, and then nodded. "Okay then, whatever you say. It was just a joke."

In the uncomfortable silence that followed, I glanced at Hugo, and when he met my eyes, he let out a breath of relief and then laughed a little.

"So, this is fun..." he offered, to which everyone chuckled.

I caught Micah's smile as he propped his chin up in his hand and looked from Josie to Hugo. He wasn't paying much attention to me, maybe he was one of those people that couldn't make eye contact with someone they thought was cute-I hoped that was the case-because I thought he was really cute. I felt tongue-tied just sitting in his presence.

And sure, I didn't get my perfect first meet-cute in middle school. No slow motion, no book dropping, no school project to kick off our inevitable love affair. But, I knew myself well enough to know that not having a perfect meet-cute wasn't going to stop me.

I just needed a clever segue.

"So, either of you have gym with Mr. Nicholson?" I asked, hoping my charm was enough for them to forgive my little outburst.

And, then, fate's design put Micah and I at a crossroads.

"Yeah, I do," Micah answered with a slight smile. "See you there?"

I made sure my eyes met his pretty chocolate ones with a flirty twinkle before promising, "Absolutely."

If that didn't make his heart race...I was doomed.

Chapter 6

There's one obvious way to seduce a teenage boy in gym class: spandex. Tight fabric stretched over our budding curves and barely covering our bottoms was the most reliable way to capture their attention. However, if you went to my school you were fresh out of luck.

Instead of letting us run around in spandex and tank tops (they knew what we were up to), they assigned a baggy t-shirt and knee-length shorts to all of the students. Both boys and girls.

Any chance at wooing the opposite sex was immediately smothered by oversized cotton shorts. Looks like Micah was stuck with my personality—something I struggled to obtain boyfriends with in the past.

But, I was determined.

After changing, we all gathered onto the bleachers to await Mr. Nicholson. All of the girls huddled together and didn't object to me joining at the edge of the group. There's a weird sort of bond between every student the moment they step into the locker room. It's silent understanding—we're all here to be judged by our ability to run lines or hit a ball over a net. It's something that disappeared the minute the bell rings.

I knew this better than anyone, so I was careful not to talk, only smile at the girls who glanced in my direction. My mouth had already almost ruined one thing today and I couldn't afford to let that happen again.

While we waited, I kept my eyes open for Micah. He was the only person I cared about—the only person I was desperate to impress. But, as the minutes drag on, I began to feel wary. What if Micah was mistaken and we didn't have class together? What if he and Josie didn't sit with Hugo and I at lunch tomorrow?

I wanted this boy. He had to be the one. I knew by the way my limbs turned to jelly when I looked at him.

Just as Mr. Nicholson barged through the heavy gymnasium doors, Micah jogged out of the locker room, his clothes slightly askew, his shoelaces untied, and his pretty brown eyes shining with urgency.

I sat up straighter and grinned, hoping that maybe my brilliant smile would catch his attention. But, no.

While Mr. Nicholson introduced himself, Micah took a seat by the boys. One of them knocked shoulders with him and pointed at his shoes, which he immediately tied up, his face glowing red. He kept glancing about nervously while attendance was being taken, but somehow managed to make his voice sound steady when his name was called.

He seemed a little frazzled, which piqued my curiosity and also put me at ease. It would give us something to talk about. I'd ask why he was nearly late for class. A genius conversation starter, if you asked me.

First he ends up at my lunch table, then I find out we share the same gym class, and now I don't have to struggle with an opening line....This was fate.

Mr. Nicholson blew his whistle and waited until all of our eyes were on him and not the pretty dark skinned boy with the glowing cheeks and crooked gym attire. My foot tapped impatiently.

"Alright kids, the objective for the day is to get to know each other. So, we're going to do some icebreakers that build trust and team bonding," he announced while he paced the floor in front of us. "We are a team here. Each and every one of you is valuable. That means, you need to branch out and see that for yourself." He stopped and looked up at us expectantly. "Partner up with someone you don't know—an acquaintance, a stranger, maybe even an enemy."

There were a few groans but, reluctantly, everyone stood and milled about to look for a partner. While they all sulked, the butterflies in my stomach flitted about excitedly. Without hesitating, I stood and made a beeline across the bleachers for Micah, who still hadn't stood up yet. Instead, he sat and watched everyone around him find a new friend.

I slid beside him and beamed when he blinked in surprise.

"Hi," I said. "Remember me from lunch? I'm Ingrid?"

He nodded. "Yeah, you're friends with Hugo. You said you had this class."

He remembered. Granted, we had discussed this was two periods ago, but still.

I bit my lip, my knees bouncing excitedly. "Yeah, I did. At first I didn't think you were coming."

"My locker wouldn't open. It got all jammed and I had to be assigned a new one," he told me, his fingers twisting around the loose fabric of his t-shirt. "Rotten luck. I barely had time to change."

I gazed at him sympathetically as he attempted to smooth and adjust the baggy cotton outfit.

Mr. Nicholson scanned the bleachers with his hands on his hips. "Alright," he called out. "Do we all have a partner?"

We all nodded.

"Good, now hop on down and spread out," he ordered. "Stay with your partner."

Micah and I followed the rest of the class onto the floor and chose an open area at the back of the room. He didn't say anything more, but I couldn't stop sneaking looks at him. I wanted him to be sneaking looks at me, too, but I wasn't wearing spandex, so what was the point?

"We are going to play a game called Baby, Backpack, Bunkbed," Mr. Nicholson told us after we all spread out. "When I call out baby, one partner is going to jump into the other's arms bridal style. When I say backpack, one of you is going to jump onto the other's back. And when I yell bunkbed, one partner is going to lie on their back and hold the ankles of the other person who is in pushup position above them holding onto the ankles of the partner lying down. You only stay with your partner and do the action once before switching. If you are the last group to get into position, you are out and you sit on the bleachers. Understand?"

I frowned. I would only be with Micah for a second before I was forced to participate with the rest of the class. The trickiest part of the game would be finding a way to partner up with Micah again without looking clingy.

"Here we go," Mr. Nicholson warned. He waited a moment for dramatic effect and then yelled, "Baby!"

My head spun as I leaped into Micah's arms, bridal style. That couldn't have been a coincidence. The stars had aligned, the signs were clear. I picked up what the universe was putting down. Micah was mine.

As I wrapped my arms around his neck and felt him cradle my back and legs, my heart beat harder than ever before. I tried to catch his eye, tried to send him a message that we were Romeo and Juliet, but he was too focused on the game.

So, when Mr. Nicholson called out the next command, and everyone scrambled to find a new partner, I squeezed Micah's arm before he disappeared completely. I was met with a confused look and an awkward, crooked smile before some girl jumped onto my back with a squeal and a high-pitched, "Sorry!"

Mr. Nicholson continued to call out commands and we all ran around the room, clinging to the first person we met. Somehow, Micah and I ended up on different sides of the gym, and no matter how hard I tried, I couldn't get us within the same sphere again. But, as more and more partners dropped out, I began to regain hope.

Bunkbed, bunkbed, backpack...

Baby was going to be called soon, and there was only six of us left on the floor. If I ended up in his arms again, he would see what I saw. He would realize the magnetic pull between us. We would look into each other's eyes and...

Backpack was called again and Micah and his new partner hesitated just a second too long. I landed on my partner's back with a sinking feeling. My prince was out.

I barely even registered the next command, and ended up losing the game for myself and a very competitive ginger haired boy, who stomped his feet and rolled his eyes at me.

I tried to reason with myself. It would have been too easy. I've never had it easy when it comes to love. It only makes sense that just as everyone was making their way back onto the floor for another round, Mr. Nicholson would tell us class was over.

As Micah disappeared into the locker room without a glance in my direction, I trailed disappointedly behind a couple girls to go change. Maybe fate was telling me to slow down and let Cupid work his magic. I did have a tendency to rush things, after all.

The notion made me feel a little better, but I was still sulking when I met Hugo by his locker at the end of the school day. I leaned against the locker beside his, staring at my shoes and not saying anything while he finished packing his stuff.

"Are you okay?" Hugo asked, his forehead creasing worriedly.

I groaned and let my head fall against the locker with a soft metallic thud. "I hate waiting."

"Ah." His brows rose and fell quickly. "Well, I don't really know what you're referring to, so..."

I lifted my eyes to the ceiling and sighed heavily. "Fate."

He snorted and hoisted his backpack straps onto his shoulders. "You're weird sometimes."

I crossed my arms as we walked down the hall. "Okay, Mister Not-Not-Sure-Not-Together. You're the weird one," I point out, reminding him of the awkward lunch conversation from this afternoon.

His cheeks burned and he shoved me lightly. "You're the one who got all mad and preachy."

"I didn't get preachy," I scoffed.

He grinned. "You did. It was weird. Especially since you were all like, 'Hugo doesn't have crushes on girls.' Thanks for that, by the way. Josie asked if I was gay, like, three times after that. I thought we were starting the year with clean slates, but now I'm just the Might Be in the Closet guy..."

I cringed. "Whoops..."

My heart sank for him. This isn't how our new lives were supposed to start. I wasn't supposed to ruin things for him before he even got a chance. But, then my stomach twisted. What if he was mad at me? This was all my fault.

"Yeah, you're lucky I'm used to being avoided," he told me, shrugging nonchalantly at the idea. "Because, if that gets around, nobody is going to talk to me."

I wasn't having any of that. I would be furious with him. How could he be so cool?

"Hugo, I am so sorry. I didn't mean to ruin your first day like that—"

He put a hand on my arm to stop me. "I just really want to get through middle school without a fuss, so don't worry about it."

"You can't be invisible forever," I scolded. He would use anything as an excuse not to put himself out there. "Middle school is a fresh start."

He shook his head, disagreeing silently.

Our hair was blown back by a humid gust of air as we pushed through the front doors and walked out to the pick-up area.

"Anyway..." he began, abruptly changing the subject while he searched for his mother's van. I was thankful for it, but also couldn't believe I was just forgiven like that so quickly. I really didn't deserve Hugo. "How was your first day? Any Possible Princes?"

The frown returned and I dragged both hands down my face, groaning. We only jumped from one subject of misfortune to the next. Thinking about both at once made me want to walk out into traffic, so I let the Hugo accident slip from my mind.

"Remember when I said I hate waiting?" I asked.

"Uh huh..."

"This one is a slow burn," I grumbled.

"Interesting," he commented, grinning. "Ingrid not being impulsive?"

I scowled at him. "I've learned my lesson!"

He waved and took me by the hand to lead me in the direction of Mrs. Guerra's red minivan.

"Well, just remember, you can jump ship whenever it starts looking bleak," he told me, being typical Hugo who doesn't have faith in anyone I pursue.

"No, he's the one," I said firmly.

Hugo dropped my hand as we reached the van door.

"I've heard that one before," he told me smugly and then popped the door open and climbed in.

I narrowed my eyes at him but didn't retort. He could be as cynical as he wanted, but I believed in kissing a few frogs. And when it comes to frogs, you have to believe in each one.

Chapter 7

After a couple weeks of staring longingly at my new Possible Prince from across the lunch table and attempting small talk during gym class I started to realize that my impatience wasn't just a personality flaw, it was a chronic problem.

I couldn't help myself from getting sweaty palms or becoming jittery whenever I was near him. I just wanted to call him my boyfriend, hold his hand, kiss his lips, and look into his pretty brown eyes forever.

I pined after boys much longer than this before it all went up in flames, but there was something inexplicably alluring about Micah. He didn't say much, but had a dreamy look in his eye. I wanted to know what he was thinking about.

On Friday while Josie and Hugo giggled about something that happened in civics that morning, I snuck looks at Micah while he listened to their story with a soft smile on his face. I was wondering how I could get him to smile at me like that when Josie changed the subject.

"So, are you guys coming tonight?"

My head jerked in her direction curiously. "Coming where?"

"Weren't you two invited?" She asked. I looked to Hugo, but he only shrugged. Josie's eyes grew and she explained, "Nina Small is having a Back to School party tonight at her house. She has a pool and her parents order endless pizza." She leaned in close and lowered her voice. "And everyone hangs out in her basement and plays Truth or Dare and Spin the Bottle."

My mouth dropped open in delight and she waggled her eyebrows. Nina Small's party, that was my chance. I looked across the table, waiting for Micah to match my excited grin, but he was too busy watching Hugo lean back in his seat.

"Sorry, Josie," Hugo said. I turned toward him in disbelief. "My mom would never let me go to a party. Besides, I'd feel really out of place and..."

"Hugo, come on. We've never been invited to something before!" I pleaded. Hugo had to agree. His mom would let him go if I would be there, and I would only be allowed to go if he came with. We were a package deal whether he liked it or not.

"Yeah, it'll be fun," Josie insisted. "Right, Micah?"

I looked to Micah hopefully. He propped his chin up in his hand and met Hugo's eyes shyly. "Josie and I will be there. It would be more fun if you came. Both of you."

I beamed and clutched Hugo's arm. "See, even Micah thinks we should go!"

Hugo flushed. "It's not really up to me, Ingrid."

"I'll sweet-talk your mom," I assured him. Do this for me, please?"

I shook his arm and gave him my very best puppy-dog eyes, something I knew he couldn't resist.

He looked at me helplessly, begging me with his eyes, but I wasn't going to let him sit inside and avoid everyone for the rest of his life. We were going to this party. I didn't want to just survive middle school, I wanted to conquer it. I wanted to conquer it by spinning the bottle on Micah and bestowing true love's kiss.

Finally, with a sigh he gave in. "Fine..."

"Yes! Thank you, Hugo!" I squealed and threw my arms around his shoulders in a grateful embrace.

Josie clapped happily and Hugo's face blazed red. I slapped at the table excitedly and Micah giggled at me. For the first time that day, we made eye contact and I grinned so hard my face hurt. I spent the rest of the day imagining how it would feel when his lips met mine.

Convincing Hugo's mom wasn't as easy as I expected. If it wasn't for Maria insisting Hugo needed a social life with someone other than me, the conversation wouldn't have gotten past "Can Hugo and I go to a pool party tonight?"

Getting my mom on board was much easier. All I had to say was that Mrs. Guerra was letting Hugo go, and I was set to sail.

"Aren't you excited?" I asked Hugo while I pinned my hair back with my favorite sparkly neon green bobby pins.

Hugo met my eye in my vanity mirror and then fell back against my mattress in despair.

"I can't believe you're making me do this," he told me tense-ly. He wrapped his arms over his midsection. "I think I'm going to be sick."

I rolled my eyes and went to sit down beside him. When his mom dropped me off, I asked if Hugo could stay and get ready with me. If Hugo was with me, there was less of a chance he'd back out.

It was no small feat getting my mom to let him in my room while I got ready, so there was no way I was letting him back out.

"Deep breathes, it's going to be fun and you're going to thank me later," I told him.

He looked up at me, face screwed up, unconvinced. "Do we have to stay long? I don't want to...you know...play Truth or Dare and Spin the Bottle. I don't even really want to get in the pool."

My shoulders sank. "Why are you being such a downer?"

He turned his face away and stared at the ceiling, mouth pressed into a tight line.

"Hugo," I probed.

He shook his head, "Forget about it, Ingrid. You want to go, so we're going."

I scowled at him, offended. "Hey," I said. "Instead of getting all weird, why don't you tell me what the big deal is?"

He glanced my way but shook his head. "Doesn't matter. You'll think it's dumb because you're so confident and every-thing. Besides, it's complicated."

"You're the only one making it complicated," I told him bitterly, crossing my arms.

He tapped his fingers against his belly for a moment. "I just..." He paused. "I don't want to be pressured into anything. I don't want people to think I'm boring...I don't want to..." He slapped his hands over his face and made a low whining noise.

I watched him struggle, quietly waiting for him to spit it out. If it was important enough he'd say it, and I could tell it was important by the way he nervously curled up and hid his face in my blanket.

Finally, he let out a breath and just said it. "I've never...kissed anyone."

The corners of my lips rose. "I already know that, Hugo."

"And, I don't want to kiss anyone tonight," he added lowly.

I lowered myself down so that I was lying beside him and looked him in the eye. "Nobody is saying you have to."

"I'm not like you," he mumbled. "You're the only person that doesn't make me nervous. I know I talk to Josie and Micah and everything but I still feel...disposable, I guess. And, maybe you're okay with that feeling, but I'm not."

I reached over and took his hand. "You're not disposable," I told him firmly.

Hugo swallowed a lump in his throat and said, "All I'm asking is that we leave if I'm uncomfortable."

"Okay," I agreed. "But you have to give the party a chance."

We smiled at each other. "Alright—since you asked nicely..."

I cut him off, "Oh, I wasn't asking. That was an order."

He rolled his eyes and pinched my fingers between his. I giggled and pinched him back.

Nina Small wasn't just popular because she was nice, she was popular because her family had lots of money. And, if that didn't make her intimidating, the fact that she was an eighth grader certainly did.

So, when we arrived at the address Josie had scrawled onto a piece of notebook paper, my nerves decided it would be a fun time to kick in.

"How did we get invited, again?" Hugo asked as we stood on the sidewalk staring up at her house in awe.

"We're really cool people who have spent most of our lives underappreciated," I explained in a voice I hoped was convincing.

Hugo's lips pursed, but he didn't try to argue with me. He stood tensely as though he was afraid one wrong move would cause him to shatter into a million pieces.

I glanced over my shoulder, but my mom's car had already disappeared down the street. She left me with her cellphone so that I could call when we needed to be picked up, but ten was the latest she'd allow us to stay and it was already seven o'clock. We were wasting time standing here.

A group of seventh grade girls appeared from behind us, giggling and talking in hushed tones as they passed us on their way to Nina Small's front door.

"Come on," I urged, pulling on Hugo's shirt sleeve. He hesitated but followed.

The door was wide open and Nina stood at the entrance greeting everyone who came in. She was a short girl with a flat nose and dark hair, and she had a smile that looked like she could be laughing.

"Hi! Pool is in the back, snacks are in the kitchen! Take your shoes off here," It was too warm and sticky outside yet for coats, otherwise I imagine she would be buried in them by now. So many shoes littered the floor at the entrance I tripped twice trying to get through.

She didn't even ask who we were or how we got invited. It was weird.

The kitchen was crowded and buzzing with conversation. A middle-aged couple, Nina's parents, flitted about refilling pretzel dishes and pointing toward the soda coolers when someone asked. They yelled back and forth at each other, their foreheads creased. I felt as though I needed make a point of thanking them later that night.

For now, Hugo and I were getting stepped on and pushed out of the way. It was survival of the fittest in here, so I looped my arm with Hugo's and shoved my way to the sliding patio doors. Outside, twinkling lights illuminated the deck and kids shrieked over pop music as they jumped into the pool.

"It's so crowded," Hugo grumbled, but I didn't know why he was complaining. He was a head taller than everyone. At least he could see the madness. My face was the one getting pressed into armpits.

I stood on my tiptoes, trying to find anyone recognizable. It was a little uncomfortable standing in a sea of people you've never met—particularly seventh and eighth graders. They didn't pay much attention to us, but that didn't make it any less unsettling.

Suddenly, arms were thrown over Hugo and I, while a perfumy, brace-faced, curly head poked between us.

"You guys are here! Yay!" Josie cheered. She turned to Hugo. "It's a good thing you're so tall otherwise I would have never found you two."

He tried his best to smile in return, but just ended up looking uncomfortable. Josie didn't even seem to notice.

"Micah is over there," she told us and pointed at a group of sixth graders sitting on the edge of the pool with their feet in the water. He was watching the water and laughing that silly laugh of his. "Did you bring swimming suits?"

I nodded. "I did, but Hugo doesn't want to swim or anything."

She bumped against Hugo with a saddened, "Aw, why not?"

"Not my thing," he told her.

She shook her head. "You're going to be saying that all night, aren't you?" She asked with a knowing grin.

"Yup."

"Fine," she sang. "But you'll be sorry later. There are some patio chairs over there," she said, pointing past the sixth graders. "Pull one up and hang out with Micah while we go change."

She gave Hugo a good push, and shooed him off. He looked back at me with a pained expression, but before I could say anything Josie pulled me into the house. Past the crowded kitchen, she led me down a hallway towards a bathroom.

We both walked in, and while I oo'd and ahh'd at the fancy glass shower door and luxurious, fluffy towels, Josie opened up a bag I hadn't realized she was carrying and started shoving her clothes inside.

"Oh, no," I said, suddenly. "I didn't bring anything to put my clothes in."

"That's fine," she said absently. "Put your stuff with mine."

Like me, she had her swimsuit underneath her clothes so changing was quick. I added my mom's cellphone and all of my clothing to her bag, and then we hurried back to the pool in our halter top swimming suits.

Once back outside, we weaved our way towards the other sixth graders. I searched for Hugo, and found him sitting in a patio chair like Josie told him to do. Micah had climbed out of the pool and pulled up a chair as well. They seemed to be talking about something that was making Micah giggle cutely. No surprise, Hugo sat back grinning proudly—the way he always did when someone found him funny or interesting.

I smiled at the two of them, happy they got along so well. Hugo absolutely despised my other princes so it was good to see him be friends with at least one, even if he didn't even know Micah was the new boy I was in love with.

Josie noticed my gaze. "They're cute together, aren't they?" She asked dreamily.

The way she said it was slightly weird to me, but I didn't ask her to explain. I wanted to go over and let Micah see me in something other than oversized cotton shorts.

"We're back!" Josie announced, and the other sixth graders looked over and waved. Among the group were a few kids I had known in elementary school, but they pretended that they didn't recognize me.

Some people might be offended, but I could only be grateful.

I went to go stand between Hugo and Micah. "What are you two talking about?" I asked.

Hugo shrugged. "Nothing really."

I frowned at the obscure answer, but Hugo only shrugged again, looking slightly lost. Micah smiled at me, but didn't try to elaborate.

"Okay, then..."

"Ingrid come on!" Josie called from the edge of the pool.

I gave one last lingering look at the two boys but they remained quiet, so I joined Josie by the pool.

My stomach flopped nervously. I didn't like being out of the loop with my best friend, and it felt even worse that he was being secretive with Micah.

What if they were laughing about me?

A wave a betrayal washed over me, but then Josie splashed my legs and I shook the idea off. I was being ridiculous. Besides, I came to this pool party to seduce Micah, and my wooing hadn't even begun.

No more overthinking.

With that, I slid into the cool water and sunk beneath the surface—wetting my blonde hair in that beachy bombshell way that made all the boys swoon.

I thought about exploding out of the water the way Ariel does in The Little Mermaid, flipping my hair back—maybe even winking. But my moment was ruined when one of the older kids did a cannonball and nearly landed on top of me. I came to the surface coughing and sputtering.

Luckily, to both my annoyance and my despair, Micah wasn't even paying attention.

And that's exactly how the night continued. I tried every-thing in my power to catch Micah's eye. I splashed and laughed loudly with other people, I got out of the pool like a chorine water goddess and ran my fingers through my wet hair. I dried off like it was a show. But, no matter what I did he just kept staring at Hugo and ignoring me.

I had never been so jealous of Hugo in my entire life.

Then, Nina announced that the pool was closed and that's when I knew my luck was changing. Now everyone would go downstairs and play Truth or Dare and Spin the Bottle and then Micah would have to notice me.

Half-dried and wrapped up in fluffy towels, a mass exodus was made from the pool to the basement.

Nina's basement was completely finished and nicely deco-rated. There was a bar on one end of the space with punch bowls and chips set out for us and a pool table on the other. Some people disappeared into the bathroom to change, but mostly kids just squeezed onto the oversized furniture or huddled in groups on the floor. The chatter was so loud that at first it was overwhelming.

Still miffed at Hugo about Micah, I stayed attached to Josie like glue. We found the other sixth graders sitting in a circle next to the bar, and that's when I realized something. Despite us being packed so closely together everyone was still hang-ing out and playing games in their own cliques and groups. The older kids barely even noticed we were there.

Getting to toss seventh and eighth graders out of my gam-ing equation, I discovered that my odds with Micah just got even better and that this could be a salvageable night.

"Who wants to play Truth or Dare?" A pretty girl with lots of freckles and crooked front teeth asked.

"Yeah, good idea, Sam," Josie agreed and rubbed her hands together like a supervillain. "Let's play."

"Anyone else?" The Sam girl pressed.

I raised my hand along with the others. Hugo was the only one who slid backwards out of the circle and kept his hand down.

I bounced my knees anxiously and looked around the circle for Micah. He sat across from Hugo, Josie, and I, and he watched Sam scan the circle thoughtfully before picking someone.

Before I could hear her ask a boy named Owen Truth or Dare, Hugo rattled my shoulder and leaned into my side.

"Come get punch with me?" he asked, his voice sounded urgent.

I scowled at him and pulled away. "It's literally right there," I told him.

"Ingrid, I really need to talk to you," he whispered.

His fingers twisted in his lap nervously. Remembering what I told him earlier about leaving if he was uncomfortable, I felt a nerve tweak sharply. The scowl I wore turned to an even uglier wrinkle of annoyance.

He just kept ruining everything.

"I want to stay," I gritted out.

He tensed at the bite in my voice, but remained persistent. "Ingrid, please come get punch with me."

With an aggravated groan, I stood. Hugo followed suit, and Josie's eyes followed us.

"Be right back," I told her pleasantly with a smile, but as soon as I turned away the act dropped.

At the bar, I turned on Hugo. My jaw clenched so hard it hurt. "What," I hissed.

He stood across from me, but the look of hurt I was expecting to see wasn't there. It was pity. "I know you like Micah," he whispered.

I blinked a few times, taken aback. I didn't know what to say to that. The way he looked at me made me feel uneasy.

"Okay..."

He shook his head. "No, not okay. You've been bending over backwards all night trying to get his attention, but the problem is he's never going to look at you, Ingrid."

I went numb, breathless. My mind stopped working, words escaped me. I just stood there, mouth hanging open, brows pulled together, and eyes watering.

Hugo had never been so forwardly cruel before, and I didn't understand why he was saying it at all.

Noticing the devastation on my face, Hugo's eyes grew and he began to backtrack. "No, no, no, Ingrid. That's not what I meant—"

"Wh—I don't...Hugo..." I choked, my cheeks blotching. Hurt bloomed in my chest and my lungs burned with each breath.

Why did he have to do this in front of everyone? I didn't want them to see me cry.

"I didn't mean that there's something wrong with you. It has nothing to do with you," he said quickly. He looked over his shoulder, but nobody was paying attention to us.

I glared at him furiously, wishing I could get my legs to move.

"What are you talking about, Hugo," I demanded.

Hugo swallowed hard and took a deep breath. "He's gay, Ingrid."

I sniffed, and choked back a hiccup. My brain couldn't—wouldn't process what he just said.

"What?"

Hugo rolled his head back and groaned. My brows stitched together, and I moved out of his reach when he tried to place a comforting hand on my shoulder. Awkwardly, he clenched both hands at his sides.

"He's been flirting with me all night," Hugo explain in a strained voice. "Josie told him I was in the closet and he's been trying to feel me out since we got here. I know you're blind when you're in love with these guys, but just think about it for a minute."

I shook my head, not wanting to believe it.

"No," I insisted. The night began flashing before my eyes. The soft smile, the giggling, staring at Hugo like he was the world, that strange comment by Josie. "No..."

Hugo shuffled uncomfortably. "Ingrid, he put a hand on my knee and told me he liked my eyes."

It clicked. All those times at lunch when Hugo was the sole focus, the way he went bashful in gym class whenever another guy complimented him.

"Oh my god, he's gay! He is so gay, Hugo," I cried out.

He nodded furiously.

"I can't believe this," I crowed, burying my face in my hands. "Why does this happen to me, why?" A thought crossed my mind and I lifted my face. "We can't stay here—not now that Micah is gay. He was the only reason I wanted to come. I wanted to kiss him tonight, but now it's not even worth the trouble..."

My whole body ached, heartbroken. Another prince to be crossed out of my book.

Hugo flapped his arms at his sides and grimaced. "I'm sorry this didn't go how you wanted it to."

"All I've done tonight is make a fool of myself," I moaned. "Are you even having fun?"

He made a face. "Not exactly. I do feel really flattered, though...because of Micah...not...you....let's not do this again," he suggested. "Honestly, I don't see what the hype is about, do you?"

I agreed with him. I really wasn't having that much fun. Everything was a show for Micah which only turned out to be a waste of time. Everything I was excited about faded from neon to white. I had no desire to be here anymore.

"I want to go home," I admitted.

An eighth grade boy pushed between us to grab a bowl of chips, barely muttering an apology when he stepped on my foot as he turned away.

Just because we were at a party didn't make us any more significant.

Hugo rocked back and forth. "Okay, sure. We can go home."

I slowly shuffled over to Josie and tapped her on the shoulder.

"What's up, Ingrid?" She asked.

"Hugo and I are gonna leave. Can I get my stuff from your bag?"

We left the group and went upstairs to change. Before heading to the bathroom, I fished my phone from Josie's bag and sent Hugo outside to call my mom and wait for me on the front lawn.

"Why are you guys leaving?" Josie asked as she unpacked my clothes from her bag.

I grabbed my t-shirt and pulled it over my damp swimsuit.

"It's kind of embarrassing," I told her honestly, keeping my eyes on the shiny tiled floor of the Small's guest bathroom.

"Oh," she said.

She fixed her hair while I pulled on my shorts. I didn't want to tell her exactly why we were leaving, but I also wanted to clear up something really important for Hugo.

"Hugo isn't gay or anything," I told her. "He just doesn't think we're old enough to fall in love."

She paused her primping and placed a hand on the counter. "Micah wasn't creeping him out, was he? Because that's all my fault. I'm sorry! I thought..."

"It's okay," I told her, trying hard to stay chipper. "It's not Micah's fault...or yours."

I did kind of blame her for this whole mess. If she knew Micah was gay and I was being as obvious as Hugo said I was, why didn't she tell me? But, I decided to keep my mouth shut. I didn't want another bad reputation following me around for the next three years.

When my mom picked us up, we drove quietly for a few blocks. Hugo stared out the window while I stewed in silence. Mom kept looking at us in the rearview mirror worriedly until she couldn't sit in the dark any longer.

"So, why did you want me to pick you up early?" she queried.

"It wasn't what I thought it would be," I told her vaguely.

Hugo snorted, confident now that the crowd was gone. "Her prince turned out to be gay."

I shoved him, but my mom didn't even notice. She was too busy cackling over the steering wheel.

Chapter 8

After the great tragedy of Micah, the boy who could never love me, things started to look up. You see, there is something fundamentally magnetic about a lovesick girl in middle school and it seems to attract other lonely preteens. And that's how Patrick Day stumbled into my comically catastrophic love life. Desperation.

Patrick Day was as hopeless as me and initially I suffered second-hand embarrassment just being around him. He had a stutter when it came to class speaking, tripped over himself and chair legs constantly, and always had a far-off look in his eyes. The guy just exuded anxiety.

"Who in our class do you think would be the first to die in the event of a zombie apocalypse?" Josie asked one weekend while were all sat on her porch listening to the All-American Rejects and pretending to do research for the science fair projects we had to finish in the next month.

"Me," Hugo replied instantly, not looking up from the book he was reading about marine life.

I rolled my eyes while Josie giggled. "Whatever, you're way too smart to die in that scenario. You'd do the smart thing and lock yourself up in Costco with Ingrid for fifty years and repopulate the earth."

My cheeks warmed and I swatted her shoulder as she cackled impishly. "Hey!"

Hugo shrugged but didn't reply, leaving me to defend us by myself.

"It would be Patrick," Micah announced over us. "I've literally watched him walk into a door that he was looking right at."

I couldn't help but burst out laughing, but that's just who Patrick was: the butt-end of a joke.

And he stayed that way until the end of the school year. That was when something happened that made my love-starved heart swell.

At the end of the school year we were given cheap versions of a yearbook. Basically, it was just a stack of school pictures stapled together with plenty of blank pages for HAGS to be written a hundred time in sparkly gel-pen. Despite this, we all thought they were pretty awesome.

I, for one, wanted to collect as many autographs as I could—you know, something to impress my older self with (as if I might forget I was a social pariah as a child). So, to start my collection I decided I needed to start small and work my way up to the popular kids.

Hugo, Josie, and Micah were the first to sign my book. That was the easy part since they were my friends. Now I needed to find the least intimidating person in school to really get the ball rolling. That person, you may ask? Well, that person was Patrick Day.

"Now would be the perfect time to ask," Hugo told me one morning before school started. Everyone was standing at their lockers, some racing against time to finish an assignment, others chatting boisterously.

Patrick was one of those people that tried to look like he was too busy to talk to anyone by rearranging things in his locker and checking inside his backpack a hundred times. Even though it was an illusion, I still felt nervous about asking him to sign my book.

I folded my yearbook over my chest and swallowed the lump in my throat. "I don't know..."

Hugo peaked at me under a mop of dark hair and raised an eyebrow. "It's just Patrick."

I frowned. "Easy for you to say. You're not asking people to sign your book."

He shrugged. "I'm not going to know who any of these people are in a couple years. Besides, you signed my book. So did Josie and Micah. That's all I need."

I sighed heavily, my limbs buzzing with intermittent shocks of adrenaline.

"Yesterday he sneezed so hard snot shot out his nose," Hugo reminded me.

The memory made me grimace, but it worked. "Alright, alright," I decided, taking a step toward Patrick. "I've got this."

The walk across the hall felt shorter than it should have. Suddenly I was standing next to a jittery Patrick Day who seemed to be humming to himself in a way he hoped would make him seem less lonely and more preoccupied.

I took a deep breath and forced a cheery smile. "Hi, Patrick."

He nearly jumped out of his skin when he noticed me standing there. I smiled like I didn't notice.

"H-h-hi, Ingrid?" He looked unsure and his voice broke. I wanted nothing more than to giggle at him but figured it would be rude, and I wanted him to sign my yearbook so I couldn't be rude.

He was tall but not as tall as Hugo, and his features were plain and round. From the curve of his nose to his lingering layer of baby fat, he was soft and squishy. Someone who could blend into crowd and get lost forever. He made a person feel much more confident in his presence, and I felt silly for feeling nervous before.

Tipping my yearbook forward, I offered for him to take it. "I was wondering if you would sign my yearbook. Maybe I could sign yours?"

He looked down at the book, dumbfounded. It was like he couldn't quite process my offer.

Finally, he mumbled, "I didn't think you noticed me."

I laughed. "Kind of hard to miss you," I told him, glancing down at all the bruises and scratches on his legs from countless mishaps with everything from his own two feet to real obstacles.

"Oh." He made a pained face. "Yeah...my mom says I just haven't grown into my body yet...so, I kind of...fall a lot..." Again, he made another face, this time more to himself.

I smiled warmly. I think he needed to see there was nothing to be embarrassed about—at least not in front of me. I was a walking embarrassment half the time too. There was nothing scary or special enough about me for him to be nervous.

"That's like my friend, Hugo," I told him. "He got really tall last summer and walks a little unbalanced now. He's better at staying on his feet, though."

Patrick laughed and ducked his head. "Yeah..."

"Well, anyways." I rocked back on my heels. He glanced up, his eyes meeting mine sheepishly. "I did notice, so you can sign if you want?"

Still looking a bit stunned, he took the flimsy book from me and held it up to the door of his locker while he scribbled his name and a message on the inside cover.

"Do you want me to sign yours, or?" I asked as he wrote.

He shook his head. "I kept mine at home. I didn't think anyone..." He looked over at me briefly and crazily enough I think I saw his cheeks flush. "I didn't think anyone would want to sign."

"Well, I would have," I told him. He handed my yearbook back. This time he seemed unable to meet my eye but his lips were curved upwards in a slight smile.

My stomach did a weird flop when I thanked him and said goodbye just as the bell rang and everyone scattered. It was like a slow-motion movie moment where everything was normal and awkward one moment and then our fingers brushed as I took my book back and that one touch flipped a switch. I felt warm all of a sudden. The boy-crazed part of my brain did a somersault at this positive interaction, and a box of heart-shaped confetti exploded all around me.

The numb realization that followed me to class made me curious to read his message, and when I did my feelings were confirmed. Patrick Day just made my Possible Princes book.

Ur the prettiest girl in our grade. HAGS. -Patrick

HAGS had never looked so romantic.

"Wait a second," Hugo blurted out. "Hold on just a minute. You can't be serious. You barely talked to him yesterday. Not possible. No way!"

I rolled my eyes and fell back against my towel in despair. Of course he didn't get it. He never got it. Love was simple and he made it complicated.

There was nothing but the tss tss tss tss sound of the sprinkler for a moment. Nothing but hot sunshine, a cool breeze, and the smell of wet grass as we laid out in his backyard.

"You're joking right?" He asked cautiously, leaning back and rolling onto his stomach to look at me.

"Hugo, do I ever joke about my potential husbands?" I ask, annoyed by the question.

His face went expressionless. "Husbands? Really?"

I groaned and turned away from him.

"Just think about it," Hugo probed. "Patrick. You guys would never talk to each other. He's shy, you have high expectatio ns...it would be a mess."

"Can't you just be supportive for once?" I grumbled lowly. "You're never supportive."

"I'm being realistic," he stated evenly.

I picked at the grass clippings stuck to my towel, trying to ignore the lecture in his voice because I hated it more and more the older we got. "You're just bitter because you never like-like anyone and nobody ever like-likes you."

That sentence tasted sour coming out of my mouth and my stomach lurched in regret, but I felt compelled to stand my ground. He always made me feel bad about liking the boys I did.

No response came, but the air felt thick between us. Curious, I turned to see his reaction, but when I leaned back he was no longer sitting next to me. I sat up quickly and looked around. The panic in my chest deflated when I realized he had moved to sit underneath the spray of the sprinkler.

His eyes closed and face tilted upwards, he sat cross-legged on the grass. Every time the sprinkler oscillated back he shivered under the rain.

He stayed that way for a little while and then abruptly stood up and sprinted back, screeching about how cold it was. I didn't understand what was happening until he got back.

When he reached his towel, he pulled it off the ground and wrapped himself in it. "So," he said casually. "What were you saying?"

He avoided looking at me and instead stared off toward the sprinkler. He was acting like he hadn't heard what I said. I took a jab at him because I was frustrated, but I must have gone too far. Because Hugo was one of those people that didn't confront problems unless he was protecting someone else. When it came to himself he ignored it.

When I realized what he was doing I felt guilty, but knew that if I tried to apologize he would ignore that too and pretend he had no idea what I was talking about.

I cleared my throat and smoothed my hair back. "'Um, I was just saying that I think I'm going to ask Patrick to be my boyfriend."

Hugo continued to stare ahead almost expressionless, but his voice was full of excitement when he said, "You guys would be cute."

Well, at least he returned supportive.

"Thanks," I muttered.

He nodded and then without warning he grabbed me by the hands and pulled me up, dragging me toward the sprinkler. Laughing and screaming, I fought against him while he held me in direct line of fire. Wet and cold we ran around the spray of the water, fighting and attacking each other with the hose until his mom called us in for dinner.

Our argument wasn't going to stop me from finding my prince. He knew me better than anyone, and my quest to find the love of my life wasn't going to stop because he didn't agree.

Hugo didn't fight me about love after that. He let me take the leap time and time again with so much as a shrug of indifference. But, he was always there when I fell too hard and ended up broken. He was the one who encouraged me keep looking. There had to be someone as good as Hugo out there for me.

On the last day of school I asked Patrick Day to be my boyfriend. Before he got to school, I slid a note in his locker that read:

I think you're cute. Do you want to be my boyfriend? Circle yes or no.

With an opening line like that, I knew there was no way he'd turn me down.

Sure enough, after school I opened my locker and the note had been returned. Yes was circled in sky blue ink. My prowess in all things love related was finally being appreciated. In that moment romance rose from the grave, my heart recited verses of Shakespeare I had yet to read, and cupid dumped a bucket of love right over my head.

Patrick Day was officially my boyfriend, and I desperately hoped there was a prince in there somewhere. A knight in shining armor he would be if he craved this as badly as me.

Chapter 9

The summer between sixth and seventh grade could have been a movie montage of bike rides, love letters, and sleepovers backed by queen Avril Lavigne's The Best Damn Thing. I survived in a permanent state of twitterpated happiness and dreamed of the day I'd get to marry Patrick Day.

Of course, nobody was as excited about Patrick as I was. Josie, although supportive, never missed an opportunity to poke fun. Micah didn't really have a whole lot of say on the matter. He mostly just giggled at whatever Josie said. My mother, on the other hand, had a lot to say about it.

Mostly it went like, "Will I ever get to see this boy?" or "Does he even exist" or my personal favorite, "Sweetie, does he even know you're boyfriend and girlfriend?"

That woman really did like reminding me of the fact that my past with boys was quite cringeworthy. But, the real reason she asked those questions was because Hugo, unfortunately, was right about this possible prince.

Patrick and I communicated almost exclusively through letters. Which, I know is pretty old-fashioned for kids living in 2008: the year technology hit us in the face with a brick.

But, that was besides the point. The point is it was so romantic I swear I felt the love Avril talked about in Hot.

It wasn't my choice to live our relationship through letters, but Patrick was a pretty awkward guy and spoke better on paper. People say you have to compromise when it comes to love. Well, this was me compromising. We had been a couple for exactly eighty-nine days and I still hadn't kissed him and made it official.

Give and take.

Mostly in his favor.

But it was working out so far, so I couldn't complain.

We exchanged letters at his mailbox and he never came outside to see me. Sometimes I'd see him in the bay window waiting for me and I'd wave.

Nothing, and I mean nothing made me want him more. I was yearning for the school year to start just so we would be forced to see each other in person.

"Do you think I should kiss him when I see him?"

Hugo and I sat with our feet in the air and our heads hung upside down while watching an old Drake & Josh rerun on my living room couch one August afternoon exactly one week before the start of seventh grade. Despite being topsy-turvy, he shrugged.

"Are you sure you're up to the challenge of catching him first?"

I nudged him with my elbow and he snickered playfully in response before sitting up and turning to face the television.

"He wants to take things slow," I explained as I too sat up and turned to face the TV. The headrush made me rock into

Hugo for a moment before straightening up, and he shook his head with a small grin.

"Maybe you're a bit too experienced for him. Maybe you need to be with someone who wants to spend time with you."

"He wants to spend time with me!" I argued a bit too defensively. "He just gets nervous, that's all. And, no offense, but I think I'm nailing this relationship, thank you."

"Okay..." Hugo trailed off. "If you say so."

"What do you care anyway?" I asked. His head swiveled in my direction and I raised my brows at him. "It's not like you're a love guru."

"I care because you want to talk to me about it," he said flatly. "Do you not want me to care? I can go back to fighting you about it if you want."

"No," I chimed in quickly. "I want you to care."

"Okay then," he said with a nod, turning his attention back to the show.

My fingers tapped impatiently for a moment in my lap. Lately, Hugo seemed to be doing a balancing act between what he chose to say to me and what he really wanted to say. Maybe it was because of that thing that happened a couple months ago, but he seemed edgy and liked to pretend he wasn't.

"Hugo," I said suddenly. He turned his attention back to me, chin down, expectant gaze. "Does it bother you that I talk about other boys with you. Is it weird that I do that?"

"Why would it be weird?" He asked, his expression unchanged and his dark eyes watching mine.

A nervous flutter made my twitching fingers pause over my skin, hovering over a spot of goosebumps.

"I don't know." I frowned at the weird reaction. "It seems to bother you."

"Nope," he promised with a large, reassuring smile. "Didn't bother me in first grade, doesn't bother me now. Same philosophy as always. Love is for grownups, and I'll keep it at that."

"You sure?" I asked. "Because when I told you about Patrick--"

"Positive," he cut me off and then stood. "I'm gonna grab another root beer. You want one?"

I shook my head, watching him disappear into the kitchen. Sighing, I turned back to the show, which seemed to have ended a little while ago. And, as my eyes scanned the coffee table I noticed his root beer was still full. When he came back all smiley with a second one I didn't say anything. I just pulled my Possible Princes journal into my lap and began rereading old love letters from the summer.

One thing I knew for sure: boys were confusing.

On the last day before school I biked the seven blocks to Patrick's house to drop off a letter that contained very specific instructions on where to meet me in the morning. As usual, the yard was void of my boyfriend. He wasn't swinging from the tire swing or playing hopscotch or reading in the bay window. There wasn't even a car in the driveway.

It had been about a week since I'd been around because according to Patrick's last letter his family was going on vacation. But for some reason the house seemed a bit too quiet for a family vacation. Maybe it was the fact no curtains were hanging in the windows or that the grass hadn't been clipped, or maybe it was the downright offensive FOR SALE sign pegged into the lawn.

Yeah, maybe that was it.

FOR SALE.

Seeing that sign felt like cupid had taken my heart, shoved it in the world's dullest blender, and hit puree.

My eyes started welling as I rolled to a stop before the mailbox. Angrily, I hopped off the bike and threw it on the curb. Knowing I would find it empty, I yanked open the squeaky metal mailbox only to be caught off guard by a pale blue envelope with my name on it.

I tore that thing open without regard for the paper cuts that would follow and gripped the letter so hard it left indentations in the paper.

Dear Ingrid,

I hope u get this letter. My dad got a job in kentucky so we had to move. I found out in june but i didn't want to hurt ur feelings so i didn't tell u. I really like u n i hope u don't hate me. I didn't want to see u cry so i decided this would be the best way to say goodbye. I don't think we can be boyfriend and girlfriend anymore but maybe we can be pen pals. Ur the nicest girl ever. Thank u for being the best girlfriend.

Love,

Patrick

And, just like that, Patrick Day wasn't my boyfriend anymore. He was nothing but eight sentences on a piece of notebook paper. He wasn't a boy waving in the window waiting for our first kiss to turn him into a prince. He wasn't a prince at all, at least not mine. He was the prince of some southern bell down in Kentucky. He had probably given my love away already.

I didn't care how considerate he thought he was being, I biked home with hate in my heart and tore up all the letters he ever wrote to me. I locked myself in my room and wailed like I just lost a limb. My heart broke for the fifth time. Three months of my life wasted on letters that would ultimately lead to a Dear John letter he knew he would have to write.

How could he lead me on? How could he let me plan our wedding? How could he leave without giving me a proper goodbye? I felt betrayed, betrayed by Patrick Day, the boy everyone laughed at. Well, now I felt like the joke was on me.

It was short-lived, hardly as romantic as I fantasized it being, and still I mourned the loss. With Avril's I Can Do Better blaring on loop, I turned myself into a blanket burrito and began to write a new entry in my Possible Princes journal. This time, I needed to establish some ground rules for myself.

Terms and Conditions of the Prince

1. Stays

2 Is, in fact, an actual boy and not a faker on Myspace

3. Isn't ashamed to be seen with me

4. Nice

5. Doesn't take me for granted

6. Believes in true love

7. Looks at me like Hugo's parents look at each other

8. Listens

9. Someone who won't make me cry (unless it's happy tears because that's a good thing)

10. Hugs better than a blanket burrito

When Mom saw the state I was in she knew exactly what to do. The more times I got my heart broken, the better she got at putting it on the mend. After a quick trip to the grocery store and Family Video I found myself on the couch with a bowl of mint chocolate chip ice cream and a Julia Roberts rom-com.

And it was during that rom-com that an idea struck me. Rom-coms were gold mines for great ideas, and this one had some pretty solid evidence to back up its claim.

After a Guerra family dinner that mostly consisted of the grownups probing the kids about how their first week of school was, Maria, Hugo, and I all went upstairs as usual. Maria immediately went to her room and shut the door so she could text her friends in peace while Hugo and I ventured off to his room.

"So," Hugo started, slowly easing himself onto his bed.

I jumped on his mattress and stood for a moment before deciding to sit cross-legged across from him. He'd been careful about what he said all week after I revealed to him that Patrick Day was no longer a resident of Michigan state, and therefore no longer the other half to my heart.

"I have a question to ask you," I proposed abruptly.

His brows furrowed questioningly and he backed up so that he was mirroring me with crossed legs and hunched shoulders.

I took a deep breath to calm my nerves because this was kind of a big deal. I trusted Hugo with all my heart, and he could reject this if he wanted to, but if it worked for Julia Roberts, dang it, why not me?

"You don't think there's something wrong with me do you? Like I'm broken or weird?" I asked.

He flipped the shaggy hair out of his eyes and sighed. "Why? Did someone tell you that you are? Did Patrick?"

"No, is isn't about anyone. Just answer the question," I said anxiously, fingers gripping the loose fabric of my jeans.

"Ingrid, you're perfectly you. What's going on?" He looked worried, nervous, like he thought I might be having a breakdown because Patrick broke up with me.

"Do you think I'd still be perfectly me in ten years?" I watched his expression intently for the unanswered, but he said exactly what his eyes did.

"I think people change a lot, but I'd still want to be your friend no matter what."

"Okay." I paused and took his hands. He looked more baffled than I imagined he would be, but I pushed through anyway. "If we're not married in ten years, will you marry me please?"

I never saw his ears turn so red in my life. Not only that, but I'd never seen him stutter over the same letter more than twice, much less five times in a row. My brain frantically began waving a red flag. The little voice in my head screamed ABORT, ABORT, ABORT.

"Ingrid," Hugo choked out. "We'd be twenty-two!"

"So?" I asked hopelessly, dropping his hands.

"That's way too young," he insisted. "You can find yourself someone way better than me. Besides, if I'm not going to be your first choice, at least make it reasonable."

"What does that even mean?"

"I don't know!"

We both back away from each other, flustered and red-faced.

Bad idea.

Hugo stood and walked to the other side of his room to glare at me, crossed arms and all.

"What?" I whined embarrassedly, face-planting the mattress so I wouldn't have to look at the completely horror-struck look on his face.

"I can't agree to ten years, that's just crazy," he said softly from across the room, his eyes flicking between the door and me. "Maybe twenty. Maybe."

I bolted up. "Wait, really?"

"I definitely think this has something to do with Patrick..."

"Only a little."

"Ingrid!"

"Hugo..."

Groaning, he dragged both hands down his face and slowly teetered back over. Seconds that felt like hours passed where he just stared straight ahead into space until finally, "Fine, I'll do it," he decided.

I beamed and threw my arms over his shoulders. "Thank you!"

"Twenty years," he reminded me. "You'll be married anyway."

I released him and sat back. He climbed back onto the edge of the bed, ducking his head so his hair hid his face.

"I hope so, but you never know," I gushed.

Hugo nodded to himself, eyes fixed on the door. "Right."

My love life was officially squared away thanks to Patrick Day. New rules, a back-up plan, and a little lesson learned about trusting boys who never want to see you in person. Now I was ready for Prince Charming. Hugo seemed convinced I'd be married well before thirty, and Hugo wasn't normally wrong about that kind of thing.

Chapter 10

The year we turned fourteen was the year my boobs came in. And not just a little bit, either. Since they popped up after a particularly long dry spell in my tragic love life, I figured it was my body's way of trying to help me out. An apology, really.

It was practically magic. Overnight it seemed my desirability among pubescent boys went from zero to ten. But, I wasn't the only one suddenly being whispered about. While I was graduating out of training bras, Hugo was thinning out and learning how to shave. And since he was easily a head taller than everyone in our class he couldn't hide. Girls were noticing.

It was weird: Hugo being giggled about. It weirded both of us out. As eighth graders, we were already inherently cool. I mean, we were practically high schoolers. But there was something absolutely desirable about eight grade boys to sixth grade girls and Hugo was no exception. While he blushed and tried to hide from the attention, I got the real brunt of it. All those brand new baby sixth graders wanted to know how to woo him, and as his best friend--and rumored "special lady friend"--I was the key.

From being cornered in the bathroom to suddenly receiving text messages from anonymous numbers, I became an inadvertent wingman and there was nothing more frustrating than that.

Where were my aggressive male callers? Sure, they could gawk in gym class and spread rumors about the probability of my sluttiness to desperation ratio, but none of them were trying to ask me out. I was over it.

I slammed down the perfume soaked, heart-covered note in front of Hugo at the lunch table before sinking down across from him stiffly and purposefully so he wouldn't miss the fact that I was upset.

Josie and Micah quieted their chatter and I could feel their gazes jump between us.

"I think this one's name is Stella," I told him sharply.

His posture didn't change. In fact, he didn't humor me with any kind of reaction at all. My brows furrowed.

Glancing up, he caught my eye and sighed. Propping his elbow up on the table, he rested his chin in his hand and looked at me tiredly.

"I told you to stop bringing me these."

"And I told them to stop giving these to me, but look how well they listen," I explained irritably. He was getting all of this attention and couldn't care less.

Hugo broke the cookie on his tray in half and held it out for me. I swiped it from him and stuffed it into my mouth angrily. Micah snickered.

"What?" I asked around a mouth full of chocolate chip.

Josie nudged him and shook her head, warning him not to--though she looked like she was on the verge of cracking a smile, too.

Micah cleared his throat and looked down. "It's...uh...nothing. Nothing. Just, um, some locker room thing about how...how much you could fit in your mouth."

"Oh, come on, Micah!" Josie whined at him.

Meanwhile, I felt as though I could sponatneously combust at any moment with the way my skin tingled and burned in embarrassment. Four months of this, and I had reached my breaking point.

"The older all of you get, the worse you get," I seethe, aiming daggers at both Hugo and Micah as though they accounted for the entire male population even though one of them was gay and the other immune to love, lust and the like.

"Boys say those things because they like you, Ingrid," Josie told me in an attempt to try and comfort.

"No," Hugo stated quickly.

Josie rolled her eyes at him but continued, "I thought you wanted them to like you."

My lips formed a thin line as I ground my teeth together. "If they liked me they would give Hugo notes to give to me." I pointed to the reeking letter still sitting untouched before Hugo. "Instead they're gross and talk about all the things they want me to do with my mouth besides kiss theirs. No thanks. Ask me out first."

"I mean, you do have a reputation for being a little boy crazy. Maybe it scares them off."

I knew Josie was trying to help, but all she was really doing was making me want to deck her. To be fair though, I wanted to pummel everyone down anyway.

I scowled. "My last boyfriend was the summer before seventh grade. Clearly, I've been unsuccessful in keeping up with my reputation."

"Ingrid..." Hugo said softly, nudging my foot under the table with his.

I looked over to see him shaking his head, telling me to settle down, that the bitter edge in my voice wasn't worth it.

"You wouldn't get it," I argued miserably. "You've practically doubled the popularity of your dad's bakery since girls like Stella found out you work there."

He looked like he wanted to smile at how dramatic I was being, but instead he just handed me the other half of his cookie and crossed his arms atop the table.

"You're being dumb," he told me. "We're done talking about it."

I clenched my jaw but didn't say anything more. Instead I just munched on the other half of that cookie, making sure to take smaller bites. Josie cleared her throat and leaned forward, dismissing Hugo's attempts to move on.

"Just curious," she began, her eyes trained on Hugo as she wrapped a finger around one of her bouncy red curls. "But, like, why don't you give any of those girls a chance?"

"The answer hasn't changed, Josie," Hugo replied while scooping peas onto his spoon, not looking up. I was half-expecting his Love is for Grown Up's speech but instead he punctuated his answer with, "None of them actually like me. They don't even know me."

Her eyelids hooded over in annoyance. "Can you stop being emo for a sec? That's what dating is for. We're in our prime, Hugo! Next year we'll be at the bottom again. Fresh meat."

"You're on boyfriend number five this year," Hugo stated flatly. "That's so much work. It's not real, why bother?"

She sighed heavily. Heavily and disappointedly and somehow far from insulted. And then her tone shifted like she was telling a secret. "It might help you out, you know."

My brows furrowed, confused. I didn't think Hugo needed love to help him, I just thought I might live vicariously through him if he found it.

"No thanks," Hugo replied. He looked up and glanced between all of us. "I don't get why it's such a big deal."

When none of us said anything, the conversation ended. Josie shrugged and turned back to Micah. I smiled softly across the table and Hugo returned it before standing up to dump his tray.

While cupid was stabbing us all repeatedly in the heart with his arrow, Hugo remained cool and unfazed. I wondered how he survived in this world at all. I felt like I was withering.

The Bread Basket was popping these days. The Guerra family bakery had always been a town favorite, but Hugo's addition to the workforce really did something for the younger costumers. He might have single-handedly been the reason obesity in our town skyrocketed around the time we became teenagers. Or maybe it was the invention of the iPad, but that's a different discussion all together.

The point is, Mr. Guerra was refiguring parts of his menu to include things like cake pops to keep kids coming back. But he didn't need cake pops, he just needed Hugo to stand at the register.

Of course, I worked there too. I kept the display cases full and mopped floors and wiped down tables. Nonna would sneak me treats when I stopped in the back and Mr. Guerra would sit on the back counter and quiz us on school work when business got slow.

It was perfect. Hugo's family was perfect. Sometimes it made me sad that my parents weren't together anymore, and then it would make me think that maybe some people weren't meant to be in love.

I was too young to be giving up.

"Ah, Ingrid. Why do you look so sad today?" Mr. Guerra asked as he handed Hugo and I our burgundy work aprons. "I should be seeing smiles. I am a wonderful boss."

Hugo wrapped an arm around my shoulder and tucked me in close. "Love sick as usual."

Mr. Guerra grinned and bowed forward to level with me. "Oh? What boy does your heart hurt for, then?"

I groaned and sunk deep into Hugo's side dramatically. "All of them."

Mr. Guerra chuckled heartily until his face turned pink and his laugh lines deepened considerably. I smiled despite myself.

"Well, how about a sweet for that hurting heart before you start?" He asked, standing up to his full height and gesturing to the sweets case.

My smile grew. "Okay."

As Hugo settled behind the register and I finished my powdered zeppole, a gaggle of young girls gathered just outside the Bread Basket's door and peeked in through the giant glass windows. I dusted off my hands and stuffed them into some gloves before picking up a tray and walking to the bread case to fill it and get a better look. As I did, the door swung open and a slender, gazelle-like girl with giant eyes and a heart-shaped mouth led her friends to the register. I recognized her immediately as Stella, the girl who tried to pass a Victoria's Secret scented love note to my best friend through me.

"Hi, Hugo," she said sweetly, leaning forward over the counter as though trying to get a better look at the menu.

Hugo smiled and tried to step out of her view so she could see better, but she pulled back quickly and turned in his direction.

"We'll all take a cake pop," she told him coyly.

I glanced between them, making eye contact with one of Stella's friends. She waved and subtly sent a thumbs up. I saved my confused grimace for when she looked away, because honestly I did not remember when I signed up to be a part of the sixth grade match-making committee. I was not condoning this at all.

Hugo signed four fingers at me from the register and I walked over to the cake pop window and pulled four separate sweets into little baggies before coming over to the register myself.

"Paying separately or together?" He asked them, remaining ignorant to the very obvious swooning emanating from the entire gaggle.

"Well, I was hoping together." She beamed brightly at him and twisted from side to side.

"Okay..." Hugo sent me a side glance. "Together then..."

"Actually," she piped up, this time really leaning forward so you could smell that Victoria's Secret perfume. "I was wondering if you wanted to go to the movies this weekend?"

His fingers paused over the buttons on the register and I watched the blush climb up his neck and ears. Oh, no. He'd lose his ability to talk now.

Mouth dropping, a word tried to escape--and he was taking entirely too long.

"Yes," I heard myself say, breaking my gaze from Hugo and meeting Stella's twinkling eyes. My stomach lurched, and I tried not to furrow my brows at my sudden outburst. "He'll go with you."

But it came out as more of a question. Shifting my weight backwards, I looked away, unable to watch Hugo's reaction.

Oh god, what did I just do?

"Really?" Stella asked, her voice bubbly like sparkling water, sweet like those darn cake pops. Practically irresistible, and my face grew hot with envy. It was so easy for her.

I heard Hugo hum, the kind of hum that comes from behind a tight-lipped smile. He was going to hate me for this.

"Cool! Saturday matinee? I'll meet you there." She told him, and plunked down a mess of coins and dollar bills for the sweets.

And just like that, the excited herd of girls chattered and shrieked their way out of the bakery. The finality of the jingling bells and the snap of the door leaving Hugo and I in a thick cloud of tension.

I licked my lips and slowly tried to back away but Hugo caught me by the arm and spun me to face him.

"Why did you do that?" He asked, his eyes wide with panic and voice higher pitch than I'd heard it in a long time.

"I don't know," I all but wailed, flinging my free arm helplessly. "It was so awkward, and you're getting all this attention and...okay, maybe I'm a little jealous and I need to live vicariously through you...please!"

"I don't want to go to the movies with her, Ingrid! I don't even know her name!"

"Stella..." I mumbled softly.

"Not. Helping."

My body felt like ice cream on a hot day, and my head was throbbing--adrenaline maybe? Was this really giving me a rush? Was I that date deprived? I groaned and pulled out of Hugo's hold.

"You don't know what it's like to be this way," I sighed dramatically, tilting my head back.

He shook his head, frowning slightly. "No, I don't. Thank God. You're being crazy."

"C'mon, Hugo. For my sake. So they all stop bothering me, please go to the movies with her. Maybe it'll be awful and they all leave you alone. Maybe it'll be great and you can understand what it's like being me for a second," I begged pathetically, tugging on his arm and leaning my forehead on his arm.

He pulled away and looked down at me like he didn't recognize who I was at all.

"I'm not going."

There was a seriousness in the way he clenched his jaw and backed away stiffly, like he was trying to hide a severe annoyance. I felt the color drain from my face and my stomach drop along with it.

"Sorry," I muttered softly. "Really, I am. It's like I blacked out for a second when she asked you out."

He didn't say anything, just quietly backed against the counter and glared down at his feet.

"I can fix it?" I offered, approaching him cautiously.

He nodded and glanced up at me. "Yeah, you can. Please. Since, you know, you're the one who said yes."

"Okay," I replied, silently bracing myself for the drama that would ensue. This day couldn't possibly get worse.

A couple more seconds of awkward tension and then Hugo stood back up to full height and positioned himself before the register.

"We were gonna go to the matinee this Saturday," he muttered. "In case you forgot when you blacked out."

Shoot.

Moaning pitifully, I collapsed forward onto the counter beside him and buried my head in my hands. "I'm the worst."

'Well, at least you have a valid excuse for backing out of the offer you accepted," he told me, voice lifting in a half-joke.

I scowled at him and though he tried to pretend not to smile, those eyes lit up far too victoriously for my liking. Try to hook a friend up in a desperate attempt to be a part of some kind if love life and you end up the weird middleman in a teen love story you'd rather jump off a cliff than see unfold in the first place. What was wrong with me? My obsession with romance was slowly driving me to insanity--and yes, I firmly believe I hadn't hit rock bottom until this point, thank you.

Chapter 11

There was no reason to be afraid of a sixth grader. None at all. Yet, there I was, standing on the outskirts of the sixth grade hallway, staring at the bubbly, gazelle-like Stella with a mix of slight annoyance and, yes...fear. Fear because I knew the wrath of a preteen girl.

You'd think with all my experience being heartbroken I wouldn't have an issue ripping off the bandage for a change, but no. No, it felt awful being the harbinger of bad news. Besides, how exactly do you tell someone, "Oh, hey. Remember that date you thought you were going on? Well, scratch those plans. I'm the one attending that movie with Hugo. Oh, also, he doesn't like you and never did. So, toodles!"

There was absolutely no way of telling someone that without ending up with a kick in the face.

But, before I could decide how to word the whole thing nicely, Stella was approaching me. Approaching me in the worst way possible too: smiling, with a skip in her step.

She had to make this so much more painful, didn't she? The universe was making me pay.

"Hi, Ingrid!" She beamed at me with a full set of teeth and looped a finger beneath the butterfly necklace resting on her collarbone, twirling the pendant playfully.

"Hi, Stella." I tried to match her excitement, but I expectedly fell flat.

"Did you come to deliver a note from Hugo?" She asked, glancing at my balled-up fists as though there might be a crunched-up message inside.

"Well, actually," I started, and she must have seen the pleasantness drop from my face because she leaned back on her heels and placed a hand on her hip like my mother did when she awaited a convoluted explanation as to why something was the way it was. Fight or flight must have kicked in because I suddenly felt very warm.

With false confidence, I inhaled a shaky breath and continued, "Hugo isn't interested in going to the movies this weekend, because, um, we—as in Hugo and I—were supposed to be going to the matinée. So, since I'm technically the one who accepted the date, I'm here to turn it down. Sorry, Stella."

Her eyebrows hiked up her forehead and she shook her head. "No."

I frowned. NO?

"Um..."

"Actually," she said, "If he really doesn't want to go, he can come turn me down himself. Okay? Okay. See you later Ingrid."

I stood dumbfounded for a second as she walked away, but then the fury followed.

I turned quickly, muscles tensing in frustration. "Stella!"

She peeked over her shoulder at me for half a second but continued walking, a couple of her girlfriends racing up beside her as the bell for first period rang.

She couldn't do that. Hugo would be furious with me. This was all my fault and Hugo would never forgive me.

Hugo stared forward coolly, the only reaction he'd had to what I told him only three minutes before.

"You know how girls are now..." I explained around a strained smile.

"Mhmm."

The rest of homeroom was quietly catching up on old homework and writing notes to pass later in class. Our homeroom teacher stood at the front of the classroom prepping her board for the day. Hugo was truly trying not to draw attention to us.

"I'm really sorry. I'll do anything to make it up to you."

"The only thing you can do now," he told me, voice soft and distant. "Is not involve yourself anymore."

"Maybe they'll all leave you alone after you say something," I tried. "Trying to ignore them has only made you mysterious."

"If I engage, I look interested." He turned to meet my eyes. "I'm not."

I sighed. "You can't escape puberty forever. Your body is already betraying you."

His eyes drooped, unamused. "It's not about puberty. Trust me. I just don't like the attention. It's weird and uncomfortable. I'm not like you. We've established this."

"I know, I know, I know..."

I knew he wasn't happy about this latest development in his newly established love life, and I felt bad—I did. But there was a small part of me that thought this was good for him. See, I had a theory that all Hugo needed was romance. If he had just a taste his inhibitions would relax, he would experience the world in color. I wanted that for him.

He needed love, he just didn't know it yet.

"You know if I confront her I won't be able to hurt her feelings," he said slowly, as though feeling it out. "I won't...be able to say no."

My eyes widened. "You mean..."

"I can barely look girls in the eye, Ingrid. I have no choice." His jaw set and his ears turned rosy.

"You're so confusing," I muttered, unable to keep my eyes from sweeping over him as though searching, calculating for answers he was too vague to give me.

"Congratulations. You get what you want."

A quick moment of exhilaration and then sinking uneasiness followed his declaration because, as always, Hugo was good at making a person feel rightfully guilty. It was his superpower.

It was around the time I had officially become a teenager that my mother seemed to dub me old enough to understand that she too needed companionship. Before this, I was only somewhat aware that she dated. I'd get dropped off at Hugo's for a night I didn't beg to stay and that's how I knew. But I never met any of her dates before that. That changed after I turned thirteen.

One night she sat me down and talked about bringing a man home to meet me. She said he was going to stay the night and that I'd be seeing him a lot. That lasted for a few months and then she came out of her room one morning and cuddled me on the couch. We watched Love Actually for the ninth time together. She ordered a pizza later that night and it felt like old times after the divorce.

That had been going on for a little while now, the Breakup Cycle as I was now calling it. In fact, Man #3 was leaning in the doorway of my mother's office that day when I came home from school. I didn't bother learning their names after Man #1, otherwise known as 'Mark.'

"Hey kiddo!" He called down the hall. I raised my hand in a wave and made toward the kitchen.

I missed when she didn't bring them around.

Both my mom and Man #3 met me in the kitchen shortly after.

"Staying at Hugo's tonight?" My mother asked me as she poured herself a cold cup of coffee that had probably been sitting there since this morning. I knew she was only doing it to make herself look busy.

I shrugged. "Wasn't planning on it. Should I?"

She shrugged back at me. "I'm not going to be here tonight. I don't want you at the house alone."

"Okay."

She smiled at Man #3 and they both smiled at me.

Weird.

"We can both have a date night then," Man #3 chimed in.

I stopped what I was doing and wrinkled my nose at him. "Hugo is my friend, not my boyfriend. He even has a date tomorrow."

Now that got my mother's attention. She nearly dropped that cold cup of coffee.

"Hugo's what now?"

"Date," I said, and this time I couldn't help the grin. "Hugo's got a date with a girl," I nearly sang.

"Does he know he's got a date with a girl?" She looked about ready to laugh.

"It's a long story, but it ends with him unable to say no, apparently. So..." I trailed off, still confused myself.

Man #3 looked between us. "So, Hugo is not the boyfriend then?"

"It's..." My mother glanced at me quickly. "I'll explain later."

My eyes narrowed at her but she pretended not to notice.

"Well, alright," she said to me. "I've already called his parents and they know you're coming. Get Hugo ready for that date, I guess."

She had this face like she couldn't believe it. And, well, I couldn't blame her, I could hardly believe it myself.

"Whenever you're ready, we'll drop you off," Man #3 told me. He wrapped an arm around my mother's waist and she looked up at him fondly.

Like Hugo's relationship with Stella, I gave Man #3 the weekend before it all went south.

I slept on the couch in the living room when I stayed at the Guerra's. Sometimes Hugo would sleep downstairs too, other times he'd stay in his room. It usually depended on whether he could stay up past midnight. If he was nervous, he'd stay up all night. And tonight, I was counting on it.

His parents had gone to bed exactly an hour ago and Hugo and I had been watching old reruns of The Office in silence. Jim and Pam were about to get together and Hugo knew how I felt about these slow burn episodes.

Nevertheless, he was restless beside me, picking at the blanket, lifting his head, setting it back against the couch, lifting it again. He must have sighed ten times now. I knew he was getting up the nerve to say something. Despite his insistence to ignore all things love and romance, he would want to talk about it. It was eating at him. He could only play it cool for so long.

"Do I have to kiss her? She's expecting me to, isn't she?" A pause. I didn't say anything, just waited because more would bubble out soon. "I don't want to. I don't want to do this. Now I have to. Why am I like this? Why can't I say no? I thought I had an out if you told her no. I mean, you were the one that said yes. But I didn't exactly say no either so...Ugh!"

He threw his head back, deep into the cushions.

"I'll just pretend I'm with you. Yeah. That'll work. Or I'll just pretend she's not there. But that's rude..."

That was enough.

"Hugo."

He lifted his head, eyes pleading.

"Just do what you always do. Keep the mysterious thing going if you want."

He turned argumentative. "I'm not trying to be myst—"

"Well, it comes off that way," I interrupted as nicely as I could. "Point is, just be you and if you feel like kissing her—then kiss her. Easy peasy. Pucker up, aim, and smooch."

"Why do you have to make everything sound so gross?" He asked, almost mortified.

"Hey," I said. "It's easy."

He glared at me. "May I remind you that your last kiss was in the second grade."

Well, that was the last reminder I wanted.

"Please don't remind me."

He swallowed and turned his eyes up to the ceiling. "Whatever, you're right. I don't have to kiss her. I don't have to do anything. All I have to do is show up."

"Exactly."

Some dialogue is exchanged on screen but I'm not really paying attention. He seemed to be gearing up to say more.

"I didn't tell my parents."

My eyebrows knit together, and I sat up. "What do you mean you didn't tell your parents?"

He pinched the blanket between his fingers and refused to meet my eye. "They still think I'm going with you."

"Hugo, they're the ones who were going to drop us off. Are you telling me I'm going to have to go on your date with you?"

He didn't say anything, and that in and of itself meant yes.

"Oh my god, Hugo!"

He sat up and shushed me, pointing up above us toward his sleeping parents and shook his head.

"Ingrid, please. I can't go alone. Just sit in the back or..."

"Hugo, that's so creepy. I can't do that!"

"Maybe, like you said, it'll be weird enough these girls will leave me alone," he explained, trying to justify.

"They'll think it's so weird they'll tell their guy friends and that effects me."

Hugo shook his head, this time more vigorously. "We're already weird, we've been weird for years. The only difference is, you have boobs, and I doubled in height. Physically, we can't keep fooling people."

He was right, I knew he was right. But couldn't a girl dream? Couldn't things change for us? Couldn't he get hit by cupid while I found my one? We seemed forever tied together in awkward hopelessness.

I didn't resent it, I just wished things were different.

"We're going to die alone together, aren't we?" I muttered in defeat.

"Thanks to your pact, I think we're stuck together no matter what." He reminded me.

We looked at each other then.

I couldn't help but chuckle. "I don't think you truly know what you agreed to back then. I'm a lot."

"I think I've handled it pretty well so far," he stated matter-of-factly.

It was a strange feeling bringing up the pact. It somehow felt like an explanation but also somehow certain. Like he knew it would come to that, and that's why he didn't bother with anyone else. It should have been a revelation, but I was too stubborn to accept it.

We had been looking at each other far too long and my skin was buzzing so I broke it off and leaned back. There was no reason to give up so early.

"I'll see a different movie than you and Stella. That'll fix everything," I finally said. "Jumped to dramatics too soon." I tried to laugh the whole thing off, but Hugo wasn't exactly going along with it.

"Right," he said. "Good idea."

All of this over some movie with a sixth grader? Yes. We were notoriously good at blowing things out of proportion and never getting right to the point. It wasn't the first time, and it wouldn't be the last.

Chapter 12

The drive to The Cosmo to meet Stella the following afternoon was never so long and painfully awkward. Mrs. Guerra had no idea her minivan was the valiant steed on which her precious prince rode to his very first date. Sweet, sweaty Hugo sat silently beside me trying to play it cool, but it was obvious to me that he was having heart palpitations.

"You two are awfully quiet," Mrs. Guerra finally broke the silence, her voice lifting a bit at the end like she was hoping for a juicy reveal.

She met my eye in the mirror and I shrugged as casually as I could. I couldn't just let her in on the secret. If anyone knows anything about Italian mothers, it's that they are smothering—and maybe that's everything you need to know about Hugo.

"What movie are you seeing this time?" She probed further.

"It's called It's Kind of a Funny Story," I replied, turning my head to watch a cluster of brown and red leaves twirl in violent circles between the tires of the car next to us.

She smiled. "Oh, a comedy this time."

"No," Hugo replied immediately. "It's an ironic title."

She tried hard not to let her enthusiastic smile falter. "Fun."

You see, Hugo had a very specific taste in movies...and they weren't exactly fun. This always concerned Mrs. Guerra.

Did I think it was an appropriate date movie? Well, it was a toss-up between that and, like, three horror movies so Stella's godawful timing was really to blame, here.

We pulled up to the theater doors in a slow stop and crawled out of the van in a hurry, Mrs. Guerra yelling her love and well wishes in the limited time between us stumbling out the door and it slamming behind Hugo.

Stella was already waiting at the doors, her pale hair whipping in the wind. When she noticed me following in Hugo's long shadow her flushed cheeks deepened and she sent daggers at her date.

I don't know why I thought I'd be able to avoid this part.

"Hey—"

"You brought Ingrid?" Her soft features sharpened into twelve-year-old fury. I shortened my steps, trying to keep my distance.

Hugo looked like he might throw up, but I don't think I'd survive Stella's wrath if I tried to save him. He had to face this dragon alone.

"We'd sort of already planned to come together so, um, she's here. But, she's going to a different movie." He managed in short, broken phrases, smiling sheepishly.

I tried nodding reassuringly, but she was determined to ignore me completely—which, you know, fair enough. I'd hate me too.

"Is she always going to be around?" Annoyance dripped from every word.

There is really nothing worse than someone talking about you as though you're not even there, but the real horror of the whole situation was having to be witness of it. I so badly wanted to disappear in the background and watch behind my fingers in second-hand embarrassment.

Hugo glanced back at me and seemed to pause, contemplating something. An internal battle between what he wanted to say versus what he should. Until finally, with a sort of renewed confidence he began to nod.

"You know what...Yeah...She is," he told her, extending to his full height. Despite the chilly wind I found myself unexpectantly filling with warmth. A smile pulled at my lips and I looked down at my feet so Stella couldn't see how happy that made me.

They shared an uncomfortably long period of unwavering eye contact, and I swear with every breath she exhaled fire, until finally she broke away and opened the theater door. Hugo met her there with two short strides and pushed it the rest of the way open for her, holding it even though she refused to acknowledge him further. With a look over his shoulder, he smiled softly and nodded at me to follow.

It's hard to explain, but there was something about the whole thing that flipped a switch in me. Hugo was always special to me, but now I was certainly fond, and I tried hard not to blush as I passed the outstretched arm that held the door for me. I couldn't say the same for poor Stella.

Hugo paid for his and Stella's movie tickets and I plunked down my cash for a separate movie ticket. Normally I would splurge on the overpriced popcorn and soda, but it didn't seem right, so before I went my separate way I handed my extra money to Hugo.

"Get Stella whatever she wants from concessions."

Hugo met my eyes with a look I hadn't seen before. Stella looked at me from over her shoulder, her expression also unreadable but almost grateful.

"I'll stop ruining your date now."

The whole dumb thing was my fault anyway--not the part where I decided to make my best friend a third wheel because I was scared of a sixth grader, but the part where I agreed to Hugo's date for him.

"Thanks," Stella muttered as I passed her to theater three, toward some nightmarish horror movie that ruined my sleeping pattern for at least six months afterward.

So, sixth grade girls stopped giving me notes to pass to Hugo after the Stella Incident of 2010. He became a dating pariah, put on multiple Do Not Date lists. And, while that would horrify most people, it sat comfortably with Hugo. It seemed to be everything he always wanted.

And after that movie date, while we waited for Mrs. Guerra to pick us up, Hugo and I sat on the bench out front in comfortable silence. Stella had left a good ten minutes ago, and the theater was almost empty now that the cheap matinee tickets were gone.

He slowly leaned into my shoulder, bumping me lightly.

"Guess I didn't have to worry about that kiss, after all." He chuckled, hunched over his lap as though he was capable of shrinking down to my height.

I couldn't help but grin at that, since this had been the definition of disaster. And even though he would never admit it, nobody wants their very first date to end up kissless. So I did what I could to salvage it by leaning over and planting a soft kiss on his cheek. As I sat back he grabbed my hand and squeezed it, his eyes lazily watching leaves skirt the edge of his shoes.

I would spend weeks debating whether it was him or the wind that gave me goosebumps then. An unsettling feeling that things were about to change nagged at the corner of my mind.

Chapter 13

The summer before high school, Hugo's mom decided that she was tired of his borderline clinical shyness. So, she gave him an ultimatum to pick a school activity to participate in or she would pick one for him. In a somewhat uncharacteristic turn of events, he decided to join a sport team, surprising everyone.

"It's fool proof," he told me as we entered a local sporting goods store to look for soccer cleats. "Only a chump would pick something like yearbook committee. This is only a three-month commitment, and almost half of it isn't even during the school year. No projects, no discussions, just minimal effort."

Hugo was a genius. I was impressed.

He picked soccer, a sport that began a month before school started, and as a freshman brought some unexpected perks. Like, for instance, he now hung around a group of other high school boys. And, because desperateness knows no bounds, if I came around to watch practice I would get to observe a small sample of the new dating pool.

I was kind of a genius, too. Hugo was less impressed.

"Have I ever told you that I think you might be crazy?" He asked in an unimpressed tone while he gathered all his gear into a bag. It was the night before his first soccer practice and he was only a little annoyed that he had to participate.

"Hugo, Hugo, Hugo," I sang, falling back onto his bed. "You have to be over the whole Love is for Grownups thing."

He scoffed and zipped his bag with exaggerated force. "It's less ridiculous, yes. However..."

I sat up grinning, ready to pounce on this little admission.

"I think what you've been doing is actually insane," he finished, and tossed his stuff aside to come sit next to me.

"Josie is worse," I pointed out defensively.

"You two are very different kinds of Boy Crazy," he told me. "Boys are like an accessory for her. You on the other hand-and don't get mad at me for saying this-you think you need a boyfriend because it's validating for you."

My features deepened into a scowl, and he put his hands up, a wall to protect himself.

"Hey, I said don't get mad, Ingrid. This is not the first time I've told you this."

I crossed my arms in annoyance. "It doesn't make it any less insulting."

He stood and went to his closet to pretend fiddle with things. 'It wasn't meant to be insulting."

I rolled my eyes and sunk back down onto his mattress. Boy, was I glad those butterflies I felt for him months ago during the Stella Incident didn't turn out to be anything. Hugo had a unique way of ruining that kind of thing. It was all circumstantial anyway, that's what I decided.

"I'm just saying-"

"Don't."

He sighed loudly, and the fiddling continued.

"Just out of curiosity," he said after a minute. "You've never, you know, felt stuff for me, have you?"

His ability to read my mind was becoming more and more horrifying, to be honest. I held my breath, but I don't know why. I caught feelings for a couple hours, and like a headache, it passed.

When no answer came, he continued almost jokingly. "I guess not, huh? I would have known about it. You're not exactly subtle."

I released the breath I was holding with an airy chuckle. Even I could admit at this point that I had not been blessed with the grace and poise of a beauty queen. Actually, I was a full-on mess. Some things you just must learn to wear proudly.

"Ah," I sighed. "Well, Hugo, just remember. You promised to marry me if we both end up old and alone so...this could all be yours."

Laughing, he must have deemed it safe to rejoin me because he plopped down next to me and laid back.

"I could handle it," he told me.

I turned my head to face him, and he looked back at me. Half grinning, with his overgrown hair stuck to his eyelashes, it almost felt like it did those couple months ago.

"But I won't have to, because I'm sure you won't need me." His eyes were sincere, and for a second my Possible Princes Journal popped into my head. It had been ages since I looked at that thing. "You know, maybe if you stop obsessing so hard it'll just happen. Stop forcing what isn't right."

And there was classic Hugo.

I patted his arm gently, the stubbornness fighting every inch of my brain that wanted to believe he had the right idea about all of this. "I just can't do that."

He snorted, clearly expecting that exact answer. "Oh, I know."

About a week into Hugo's soccer season, I figured I'd given it enough time. If I showed up to watch a practice here or there I wouldn't look like a weirdo. So, an hour in, I walked the five blocks to the high school athletic fields and took a seat on the aluminum bleachers where their water bottle and bags littered the first two rows.

Excitingly, I was noticed almost immediately. Every couple minutes one of Hugo's teammates would glance in my direction, either trying to get a good look at me or make sure I wasn't riffling through their things like a thief. But really, the only thing I intended to steal was one of these jock's hearts.

These last couple of years I looked less and less like a little kid. Obviously, because it got me the bad kind of attention last year. But I was a little taller now, and my weight was better distributed. My mom agreed to let me wear more makeup and I mastered the art of a messy bun. My glow up years had officially begun, and I knew it. Sexy and I Know It? There had never been better timing for the release of that chart-topper.

After watching him kick the ball around (well, stumble over it) in a game of scrimmage, Hugo jogged over to the bleachers and snatched his water bottle.

"Welcome," he greeted me breathlessly. He only had the energy to look half as unimpressed with my antics as he normally does. I just smiled widely and knocked my knees together.

Running a hand through his sweaty hair, he looked over his shoulder to see if he was being missed and then back to me with relief.

"They're talking about you," he told me and squirted more water into his mouth.

"Really?" I gushed. At least the sunburn was worth it.

"Yep." He nodded. "I hope you enjoy such names as Hottie with the Bangin' Body and Blonde Goddess, because I've gotta tell you, I'm beginning to feel like punching someone. Maybe it's the testosterone from all this godforsaken exercise, maybe it's the heat, but I can't stand it anymore. Are you going to stay?"

By the end of his rambling, his eyes were hooded in complete annoyance.

I couldn't even respond. Blonde Goddess? I took a mental picture of this moment, framed it, and hung it in the part of my brain where it would always be illuminated by sunshine and good feelings. Flattery won my heart every time. I wanted to marry all of them. Frog Girl who? She was dead.

"Stop looking at them like that," Hugo begged, as I stared off at all of them, entranced. Sunbaked, glistening with sweat, out of breath, and in full adoration of me.

If someone told me this is how high school would start off for me, I would accept every previous garbage interaction with boys without question. This is how I always wanted it.

"Ingrid, I can see the drool. Frankly, I'm disgusted." He set his water bottle down with enough force that it rattled me out of my trance.

He crossed his arms and raised his eyebrows, but I couldn't stop the giggle.

"Hugo, coming here was the best decision I've ever made."

He groaned and turned away with a flat, "Bye."

I could tell he was amused, though. He wouldn't come over and tell me all that if he wasn't expecting some ridiculous response. When he rejoined the group and a couple guys high-fived him and looked my way, I knew he had probably gotten some props. So really, he'd thank me later.

At the end of practice, when they all came over to get their stuff, a couple of them made eye contact with me and said, "Hey," with a friendly smile. I blushed so hard I swear my whole body turned pink. And then Hugo waited for me to climb down the couple steps and we walked together to his mom's minivan.

"There was too much thirst on that field today," he said, adjusting the strap on his shoulder. "I have a feeling I'll be seeing that journal again."

I pushed him playfully and bit my lip.

"That felt really good," I admitted. "I said middle school was a fresh start? That was too soon and way too hopeful. No...high school is it."

"Uh huh..."

"Finally."

He opened the car door for me and we both climbed in.

"Hello, Ingrid," Mrs. Guerra greeted me in surprise. "I didn't know I was picking you up here. Your mother didn't say anything..."

"I walked over here to watch Hugo's practice," I explained quickly. "Sorry."

She looked at me through the rear-view mirror, her eyes smiling like she knew what I was up to. "That's alright, sweet-ie. Am I dropping you off at home?"

"Yes, please."

"She's got twenty new boyfriends she's gotta call," Hugo teased.

I glared at him. If his mother wasn't there, I would have squeezed that water bottle he held right in his face. She only laughed, though, and pulled out of the parking lot. So, I wasn't too mad.

Hugo was right, though. A couple of them did catch my eye, and for the first time I think I finally caught theirs.

I could never be the girl to sit back quietly and wait for love to find her, as Hugo suggested. That wasn't me. I had to hunt it, find it, make it mine. I wasn't subtle, and I wasn't good at reading subtle. If I stopped obsessing and searching, I would never see it. So, if love was truly already staring me in the face, it really had to make itself more obvious. Obvious, like the boys on Hugo's soccer team. It didn't keep me guessing, and I liked that.

Chapter 14

I continued to pop into Hugo's soccer practices, probably more often than I should. It recharged my confidence every time one of those sun-kissed, lanky teenage boys smiled in my direction. I knew it shouldn't, but it did. I basked in it.

Was it making me wear low cut tank tops and booty shorts? Perhaps.

Was I a little ashamed of my embarrassingly urgent need for attention? Absolutely.

Was there anything I could do about it? Nope. Every part of me screamed to not let this moment go.

So, I continued parading myself around the soccer field. I even accepted the name Hottie with the Bangin' Body. And if any of them decided to say it to my face one day, I wouldn't even pretend to be offended. I'm not even sure I would tell them my real name.

Hugo, of course, was being Hugo about this.

"Could you please wear a shirt that covers your areolas, please? And, for the love of everything sacred and holy, the less buttcheek, the better. I don't want to see that. My coach doesn't want to see that. Only the perverts want to see that.

You're projecting a bad image, I hope you know. I love you, but I'm going to have to forbid you from coming back. I don't want to hear another jerk-off story, Ingrid. I will kill myself if I hear another jerk-off story."

All dramatics.

I mean, of courses I was a little disgusted, and I really didn't want to know about the jerk-off stories either, but there was a positive coming out of this. I could just feel it.

On a particularly hot day in the great Midwest, a day that warranted the tank top and booty shorts, one of Hugo's teammates finally decided to make a move.

"Hey, Sunshine," one boy said to me as he jogged over to the bleachers to drink from his water bottle.

But, I couldn't really call him a boy. No, this was a guy. Some intermediate hybrid between boy and man. He was athletic and skinny with blond corkscrew curls and bronze skin from all that sun. I could tell he was an upperclassman from his build, and that just made my heart pound more. Pale blue eyes met mine, and like some movie magic I couldn't even comprehend, two beautiful dimples appeared framing his smile.

I nearly passed out from the shock.

"Hi," I said softly, suddenly as shy as Hugo.

He stepped up onto the bleachers and bent over, holding out his hand. "I'm Corey. I'll be a junior this year. You're Guerra's friend, right? Freshman?"

"Yeah, my name's Ingrid."

"Cute," he said, stepping back down.

God, I wanted to die. In a good way. My body felt a thousand pounds heavier, and I couldn't even feel my face. What was my face even doing? Smiling? Wincing? Twitching? Who knows? Not me, that's for sure.

"You wanna get some ice cream after practice?" He asked, lips pulling into an amazing half-grin. He knew I was wrapped around his finger. And honestly, I was into it.

I had plans to get a ride with Hugo and his mom, but that quickly went out the window. If this guy drove me home? I'd probably cry with sheer, unapologetic joy.

"Sure," I said, careful not to sound too eager. It was taking every last shred of self-control I possessed to not tackle him.

"Cool," he said, taking a couple steps backward. Then, "Don't go anywhere." And with that, he turned on his heel and rejoined the team for some drills.

As soon as he was out of hearing reach, I released a quiet scream and giggled. High school. This, I could get used to. What kind of alternate universe had I crossed into?

After practice finished and they all scattered, some sending smiles my direction, others nudging Corey, Hugo grabbed his bag and waited expectantly at the edge of the bleachers.

I stood and hopped down.

"I'm getting ice cream with Corey," I told him.

His eyes widened. "You're what now?"

I bounced a little and rubbed my sweaty palms on my shorts. "I think I'm going on a date."

He just stared. "Does your mom know? Won't she be expecting you? What about work?"

"She's with the latest boyfriend. She thinks I'm going home with you after practice, which, you know, is what I have been doing." I said, like I shouldn't have to be making things clearer. "Besides, the date will be over long before I have to be at The Bread Basket."

"My mom's going to tell your mom that you didn't come home with us," he told me, frowning.

This was starting to feel like a fight. It really wasn't that serious. "It's not a big deal, I'll tell her later. She's busy."

Corey came up behind Hugo and waved at me. I smiled, and Hugo jumped when he looked over his shoulder and saw him standing there.

"Jeez, you're quiet," he muttered to himself, and then looked back to me. After a second of battling some internal dilemma, he conceded. "Alright, then. Have fun."

Corey patted him on the shoulder. "I'll take care of her. It's just ice cream."

Hugo kept his eyes on me but forced a laugh. "It's cool. Just making sure she's good. I'll see you later."

I gave him a reassuring look and both Corey and I waved as he reluctantly walked toward his mother's minivan.

When Hugo was far enough away that I felt comfortable, I met Corey's eyes hesitantly. "So," I said, bouncing on my toes. "Ice cream?"

He grinned and nodded for me to follow. "Ice cream."

I followed him across the parking lot toward a silver jeep and waited for him to throw his bag in the back. Sure enough, like a true gentleman, he walked me to the passenger side door and opened it for me. I tried not to look too pleased.

"Thank you."

"You're very welcome."

The butterflies in my stomach were going crazy. Never had I gotten the Girlfriend Experience from any of my previous love interests. This was an entirely new thing, and already he was going above and beyond my expectations.

This time I was sure. He's the one.

"So," he said as he slid into the driver's side next to me and started his car. "Dairy Queen or Cherry on Top?"

"I think it's obvious," I stated, feeling incredibly smooth.

"You're right. Cherry on Top." I think the grin on his face was wider than mine.

I squeezed my hands together in my lap. Was I really doing this? Was this happening? I was sitting in an upperclassman's jeep. He was gorgeous and smelled like grass, sweat, and powdery deodorant from a morning of athletics. His smile was brilliant, and he opened my door for me.

My whole body was in Red Alert: hot, fuzzy, clammy, with the bonus of a full-body blush—and no, it wasn't the sunburn.

We pulled out of the parking lot, and as we did, he put his free hand on my knee. It didn't feel offensive or weird. He didn't seem like the kind of guy who was gross, just incredibly confident. And since I was in Red Alert, my whole body wanted to catch on fire when he did it.

"You don't mind?" He asked, just to be sure. That right there sealed the deal.

"I don't."

"Cool," he said.

"Cool," I echoed back.

I smiled like an idiot, and from what I could see from my many not-so-secret glances, so was he. A victory in itself. I'd never been this lucky in my life.

"You must really like soccer, huh?"

I had to look like a tomato at this point. Jeez, how was I going to break it to him? If I said yes, he'd try to ask me questions I couldn't answer. If I said no, it was a dead giveaway that I was a creep. I've seen the movies, I know how this goes.

I grimaced. Well at least there were twenty other potential suitors who had me on their radar if this whole thing didn't work out.

"Well, no, not really," I said honestly.

He chuckled and squeezed my knee. "Just supporting your friend, then?"

I looked from him out of the corner of my eye and noticed that look. The kind of look you wear when you think you know something that the other person doesn't think you know.

Oh, but now I knew he knew.

Humming, I tried to relax every part of my body. You know, be casual. Play it cool. Scream internally.

"You guys don't mind that I come."

He bit his lip and slouched back in his seat. With a nod he met my eyes, and I hoped he couldn't feel my goosebumps under his hand or see the smug look on my face. It was taking a lot of my concentration to appear chill.

"Alright. We do make it pretty obvious." He lifted a finger from the steering wheel, preparing to make a point. "But, when someone says 'cute girl in your five o'clock' it's hard not too look. Some of those idiots looked over their shoulders so fast they gave themselves whiplash. It's just not discrete."

"Well, I was trying to make you guys look. So, sorry about the whiplash," I said. My lungs tightened, like my body was trying to reject this sudden wave of confidence. How do people ever stay humble when they hear stuff like that?

"It's cool. Makes us work harder when you're there."

God, he was really laying it on thick. No one ever said this kind of stuff to me. No one ever approached me. I did all the work, not the other way around. It was odd. Had I finally shed my childhood embarrassments? Was this my new life?

My mind reeled as we pulled into the parking lot beside the ice cream parlor. We walked together to the shop, and as we neared the door he placed a hand on my back and leaned forward to open the door for me.

I wondered if it would be socially acceptable to literally swoon.

He ordered a sundae and I ordered a strawberry milkshake, and then we picked a retro style table in front of the window to sit.

"You ready for high school?" He asked as he picked the cherry off the top of his sundae and twirled the stem between his fingers.

I shrugged, watching his lips wrap around the fruit. "I guess so. Hugo and I usually stick together, so I'm not dreading it really. He's the one to worry about. He gets really anxious about learning the new building layout, and the cafeteria situation, and teachers."

"Yeah, he's a pretty nervous guy. Have you noticed how his first instinct is to run away from the ball when we kick it at him? He asked quizzically. "Him being so tall, it looks goofy. For his sake, we leave him as a last resort. It's an unspoken agreement between him and us."

I giggled and he watched with amusement.

"Have you ever had braces?" He asked, pointing to my teeth.

I shook my head. "No, it's the little gap between my front teeth, isn't it?"

"Yes!" He sat forward while I smiled for him. "It's adorable."

I covered my face with my hands and leaned back, feeling overwhelmed. This was too good to be true. And while these days I was more cautious, that didn't mean that I wouldn't fall completely and foolishly for him. Because I would in two seconds if he said the right thing.

"Are you serious right now?" I asked, hands still over my eyes. "Are you a real person?"

"You're so pretty, Ingrid," he said, his voice softening. "And from the little conversation we've had, I can tell that you're funny and you're smart. I really don't know how you're single, but I'm not going to give anyone else the opportunity to change that."

I peaked through my fingers at him. His forearms rested on the table, a genuine curiosity shone in his eyes, and the confident grin from before had faded. He was so easy to trust.

He was the one.

And from that point forward, he had my heart. How could I pass that up? Maybe I had gone about this the wrong way, you know, with the cleavage and the booty, but it all felt very justified now. This is the most self-control I've ever had. I could reward myself now.

Before, I would go on about how heart-shaped confetti sprung from my soul and God himself descended from the heavens to declare to the world that this was true love. That just isn't how it felt this time. This time it felt like an adrenalin rush. It felt real and grown up.

This time I didn't want to tell Hugo.

Chapter 15

"So," Hugo prompted as I adjusted my apron behind the counter at his family's shop. "How was your date."

I glanced at him reluctantly, but he wasn't really looking at me. He leaned on his elbows and fiddled with the pens beside the cash register, trying not to look as interested as his voice let on.

I swallowed thickly and stuffed my hands into some plastic gloves. It was hard to act normal, I almost felt guilty.

Gush about Corey. Do it!

"It was perfect." I smiled quickly in his direction and took a couple steps toward the kitchen, pretending to check for fresh pastries or bread. "He held the door open, paid, you know...He's cool."

Hugo stood upright and turned to me, his brows furrowing.

"It doesn't sound like it was perfect," he commented curiously. "I was expecting a Shakespearean sonnet, uncontrollable giggling, something more Ingrid. This is the man of your dreams, after all."

I looked to the ceiling for answers written in the tiles and frowned when I couldn't pull an explanation out of thin air. I couldn't even explain it to myself. It made no sense. I had everything I wanted. Corey and I agreed to see each other again, I had been dubbed a blonde goddess, and everything else was pretty much perfect. This wasn't one of those deluded scenarios of the past. Things had never been more real. So, why couldn't I tell Hugo? Why wasn't I excited?

"You don't really want to hear about it," I heard myself say, catching his gaze with mine. It held for a moment, his warm eyes sharpening before turning away.

"It's your favorite thing to talk about. I'm used to it," he said carefully and pushed away from the counter. He looked back to me, his shoulders gathering around his neck in the old Hugo way that he thought made him appear shorter.

I snorted. "You always say that, but I know you don't mean it." He rolled his eyes, but I cut him off before he could say anything. "I know you're going to be a buzzkill. Corey is it, Hugo."

A frown pulled at his lips heavily, and after a swallow he nodded. Hugo was hardly one to argue, and his eyes had sort of glazed over as his thoughts turned inward.

"Okay," he said, shortly. "You're right, I didn't want to hear about it anyway."

My eyebrows pinched together, and I could feel more guilt bubbling up. He only ever tried to be a good friend, and it felt wrong to pull away any conversation of Corey, like I was blocking Hugo out of my life. But inside, I knew it was the only way I could make things work with Corey. The less Hugo was involved, the less tense our friendship would be. I decided a long time ago that I shouldn't have to sacrifice my friendship with Hugo for a boy. This was my solution.

"I just don't want things with us to be weird because of Corey," I tried to explain.

He laughed to himself and ran a hand through his moppy hair, shrugging as his hand fell away from his head. I could see his mind working behind all his fidgeting. "You just made it weird, Ingrid. I don't want to hear about the losers because watching your heart break isn't fun for me." He paused, glancing at me quickly. "I think Corey actually likes you. If you don't talk to me about him, we'll never talk again. Things like this consume you. I get that. Don't block me out."

I frowned now, too. "You're just going to get annoyed with me."

"Ingrid, you love without a sense of caution. I say what I do to protect you. That's not going to change. Ever." His voice was stern, suddenly very grown-up. "The only time other people have come between us is when you let them. I'm always right here."

I bit my tongue at that. It was impossible to argue with him, always had been. You might think you were the most rational person in the room until he opened his mouth. But it made me scowl, because he wasn't letting me do something for him. Maybe the guilt I felt was a sadness for putting Hugo through this again. I was only trying to help. Yet he fought back calmly, logically somehow, though his voice was almost accusing and...jealous.

"You know," I said, pointedly. "'We only ever fight about boys."

He went very still, and I let out a breath of annoyance. Just that one breath, and I missed the subtle flush of his cheeks and hard swallow in his throat. I looked down at my feet.

"I was just trying to spare us the fight."

"Fine," he said softly. "We don't have to talk about it."

And for the rest of the shift we tiptoed around it. I think it was more weird and awkward to do things my way, after all. But I was stubborn, so I kept my musings and daydreams to the Possible Princes journal and Hugo pretended he didn't care.

Corey and I hung back the next day after practice and laid out on the soccer field side-by-side. His fingers brushed against my wrist and the smell of mowed grass made me feel like I was in some indie romance film. I smiled to myself and turned my head to look at the perfectly tan, gorgeously handsome junior beside me. Again, I wondered what planet I got dropped on that made this guy think I was worthy of him.

"Hugo talked to me today," Corey said, his eyes tracing the lines of clouds passing above us.

That made me rise onto my elbow in a panic.

"Shoot, he didn't say something totally weird to you, did he?" I asked. I didn't even notice them talking. I had been at practice all morning, I had watched both Hugo and Corey run around the field, break off for water breaks, gather their bags. Not once did I see them talk to each other. Just leave it to Hugo to take matters into his own hands.

"When we were setting up this morning, we were setting out cones together and he got all serious and was like, "Ingrid likes you a lot, please don't break her heart." It wasn't weird, it was just out of nowhere." He scratched his chin and tilted his head my way. He had gorgeous deep-set eyes that threatened to hypnotize me.

"Sorry about that," I started, and bit my lip. It was nice of Hugo, really, but embarrassing. "He just worries about me."

He shrugged dismissively. "It's fine. I don't want to freak you out but that guy is, like, in love with you. You can tell by how protective he is."

He watched my face as I took in the information. It didn't really phase me, though. Josie had been teasing Hugo and I for years. It wasn't anything I hadn't heard before, and it wasn't anything I believed either.

I mean, Hugo? He was the king of platonic relationships. He got uncomfortable by the idea of romance. Besides, he knew I was on the hunt for my prince charming. So, if he was in love with me, why wouldn't he just say something?

"No, no. We're friends, it's not like that. He doesn't like anybody. Never has," I assured Corey with the sweet smile I had practiced all last night in the mirror.

He still watched me, as though inspecting how I formed each word, listening to the fluctuation of my voice. I had a feeling he thought I was trying to cover something up. No one ever payed that much attention before, and it made me body buzz with excitement. If Corey was jealous of Hugo, it meant I was worth something. I was valuable.

After a moment, his gaze relaxed, and he smiled back. "You sure?"

"Positive."

"Alright, then." And with that, he reached up and pulled my face down to his.

I remember my first kiss under the slide in the second grade. It was quick and soft, like hummingbird wings. I thought I missed it. But, my first real kiss was entirely something else. It was firm and soft at the same time, his lips slid between mine effortlessly—like he'd done that exact trick hundreds of times. And he held me there, breathing me in. There's no way I could mistake it as anything else. I thought it was that transforming, magical kiss. The one that secures forever. In my mind were fireworks, brightly colored and glittering. It sealed the deal, locked me in.

He loosened his grip, and I leaned back. I was glowing, innocent. I looked into his perfectly lovestruck face and I was sure I was staring into the eyes of my prince. He seemed to glow too.

"So," he said. "Do you want to come to the bonfire this Friday. It's the last Friday before school starts and the team is throwing an end of summer party. A little spiked punch, a little cozying up around the fire. Maybe we sneak off behind the haybales, do a little more of...that..."

He grinned suavely, and I couldn't form the words that would give him an answer. So, I nodded enthusiastically and giggled as I fell back into another kiss.

Corey dropped me off at my house later, and luckily, my mother wasn't there. She still wasn't aware that I was hanging out with an upperclassman and having his tongue shoved down my throat in the middle of the soccer field, but I knew that if the Guerra's had anything to do with it, she would hear about it soon. Besides, there was the matter of the bonfire on Friday.

I couldn't see that suggestion going particularly well...at all.

Hey mom, can I go to this high school boys soccer team bonfire on Friday? It's at some guy's parent's house on the outskirts of town. I don't know when I'll be back, but I shouldn't be too drunk. Oh, did I mention the entire team thinks I'm a star-studded Hollywood babe? It's all thanks to your glorious genetics. Toodaloo!

Yeah, that'd go swimmingly. Couldn't imagine how I wouldn't be rejected.

But I had to go. Corey invited me. It was an exclusive soccer team bonfire. The last time I went to a party was a middle school nightmare. A waste of a night. An embarrassment. This was a glow-up if I'd ever heard one. So, I was going.

I just had to formulate a plan that would give me the green-light. Unfortunately, I knew exactly what had to be done. And Hugo was going to hate me for it.

My mom showed up an hour after me, and kicked her pumps off at the door. She walked barefoot into the living room and lifted my feet so she could sit on the couch beside me. I let my feet fall back onto her lap, the fabric of her pencil skirt was cool and slippery.

She leaned her head back and watched Keeping Up with the Kardashians with me for a minute while she decompressed. After this, when she was still tired but less frazzled, that was the time to strike.

I thought I was slick, eyeballing her out of the corner of my eye, but she turned her head to me, her face expressionless, and in heavy monotone asked, "What?"

I tried to smile, real coy-like, but her eyebrows only perked up.

"You're up to something, Ingrid Owens, and I don't like it," she pressed.

I sat up, and began pleading. "Mom, Hugo's soccer team is having bonfire this weekend, and I really want to go. It's important."

"His high school soccer team—of boys—is having a bonfire and you want to go?" She asked suspiciously. "Tell me how you fit into the picture there."

I tried to appear casual, dropping my eyes to the couch. "There's a boy on the team that likes me and asked me to go with him..."

Her eyebrows somehow slid higher up her forehead and then she chuckled to herself and sighed amusedly. "Oh, is that it? You want to go to a party with a boy."

I nodded and quickly added, "Hugo is going to be there."

"Uh huh." She pressed her fingers to her hairline and let out a deep breath. "Oh, Ingrid, I don't know."

"Adults are going to be there, Hugo is going to be there, Corey..."

"Corey. Is this boy you like?" She guessed. I nodded, hope gleaming in my eyes.

"Tell me about this Corey," she proposed. "I want to know why I should trust my daughter to hang out with him."

I wanted to roll my eyes, groan, but I couldn't. This was a delicate situation. Only severe politeness and well-practiced begging would get me the answer I wanted.

"He's a junior. He took me out for ice cream yesterday and held the door open and paid. He always asks if what he's doing is okay. He just wants to show me off and cuddle beside the bonfire with me. It's going to be fun, please!" I dipped every word in sugar, as if my mom hadn't played the same tricks decades ago. If I believed hard enough, my wish would be granted.

"Sure, and Hugo? What about him?" I think she truly believed Hugo couldn't get along without me. I mean, she wasn't wrong, we were a package deal, but I would deal with that later. Or maybe she knew I had made plans without Hugo's approval, and well, that was the truth.

"Those are his teammates," I told her. "It's not like I'm going to ditch him, though. The last time Hugo and I attempted something like this, it didn't go well. Redemption, Mom. Redemption."

Now that made her laugh, the memory blooming in her mind. Hugo and I in the back of the car, our faces of disappointment. It seemed to make up her mind.

"Alright, you can go. But Hugo will be there. His moral compass is true enough to cover the both of you."

I nodded at that, heart swelling. I sprung up and wrapped my arms around her neck.

"Thank you!"

She patted my arm and waited for me to release her. Then she adjusted herself to face me and placed her hands in her lap.

"Now, let's refresh on the birds and the bees," she stated calmly, but the amusement in her eyes lit up when I recoiled and muffled a shriek of horror.

"Mom! Mom no!"

"Also, since we're going to talk about this, you're in high school now. If you want to go on the pill, we should talk about it. We don't want any surprises. And no matter what he says, the pull-out method is the dumbest thing to rely on. Are you really going to trust his accuracy?" The worst part was how perfectly at peace she was. Meanwhile, I was cringing. I couldn't even look at her. I wanted to die. "You're old enough that I can't stop you from doing what you want, I'm just here to offer my wisdom and advice..."

I pressed my hands to my face and stifled a cry for mercy. I should have seen it coming. I should have known I'd be subjected to the talk. I wasn't even thinking about sex, but she was older and wiser. She knew the mind of a sixteen-year-old boy. She had once been a teenage girl. I couldn't decide if this tradeoff was worth it. I should have just snuck out like a normal teenager.

Chapter 16

The news about my new boyfriend spread like a flu virus among family members. The night after, at our weekly dinner at the Guerra's, I was bombarded with questions. Mr. Guerra even pinched my cheeks as though it was precious. "So cute," he sang, his cheeks red and eyes sparkling.

I adored the attention. The way I talked about Corey would make anyone believe I was describing a chivalrous knight. I had been a lovesick damsel and he rescued me from my tower of loneliness. My mother rolled her eyes at my colorful storytelling while Hugo shook his head and pushed food around his plate. His family leaned in and cooed over me. I basked in it.

Afterward, as we all cleaned up, Nonna approached me at the sink and placed a hand on my arm. "New love," she said in her thick accent, her wrinkled eyes crinkling at the corner. I nodded. She smiled affectionately at me and squeezed my arm. "One day, true love."

I smiled back politely, puzzled, and accepted a toffee from her apron pocket before she stepped away. Hugo came up behind me and dropped some silverware into the sink.

"See, you should have just told me about your date. I heard the whole journal entry in there," he teased, nudging my shoulder playfully, pretending we hadn't had a whole awkward blowout over this a couple days ago.

I wrinkled my nose and turned to face him, finding him surprisingly close. I decided to cross my arms. "You probably hated every second of it."

He set his plate down on the counter beside us and sighed lightly. "Well, if you're going to bait me into admitting it..."

I pushed him back gently and grabbed his wrist to lead him out of the kitchen. Well, if we were acting cool again, I might as well break the news to him.

"Thanks for dinner, Mrs. Guerra," I called as I pulled Hugo up the stairs. She called back from the dining room, but I didn't catch it. Hugo was talking.

"I know what you're up to," he said, pulling his hand away. We stood at the top of the staircase and he backed against the wall, a smug smile. "Corey told me this morning that you're going to the bonfire with him. There's no way you're going if I'm not there too. Your mom would never let you."

"Oh, good. I thought you were going to throw yourself down into the depths of despair over it," I admitted, rocking backward. But, I knew Hugo—and I knew that smile. He wasn't saying yes, he was just pointing out what he knew to be true. "You don't want to go."

He took a breath and pushed away from the wall, leading me into his room. "No, I don't. But I know I'll give in if you beg."

I sat down next to him on his bed and crossed my legs, listening closely. Was he saying yes? My lips began to twitch into a victorious smile.

He put a hand up, freezing a half-smile onto my face. "I'll say my piece even though I know it makes no difference to you." I tried to argue that it wasn't true, but he put his hand up again. "You don't hear half of what they say about you. I do. I know Corey really likes you because he doesn't join in...But he doesn't tell them to stop either. All I'm saying is, be mindful. They think you're something you're not."

I pick at his bedding and purposely avoid eye contact. "I know what they say..."

"And you don't care?" He guessed. He knew me too well.

I shrugged. Hugo didn't understand. He never would. You had to put yourself out there sometimes. I'd rather do what I did than sit back and hope someone noticed me.

"I have Corey."

His jaw clenched for a moment and he nodded. "Right."

Hugo worried too much. He thought my Myspace boyfriend (girlfriend?) was a forty-year-old creep. He always assumed everyone was trying to manipulate me or use me. Something Corey said the other day rung in the back of my mind. Hugo was very protective.

"So, are you saying you'll go or...?" My eyes glittered with hope. I couldn't do this without him.

"Unfortunately..."

I leapt into his lap and threw my arms around his neck, squeezing him into a tight hug. "Thank you, thank you, thank you!"

I felt him release a breath, and he seemed to reluctantly lift a hand to pat my back. "I have stress ulcers because of you."

I pushed away from him and rolled my eyes. "So dramatic."

He scoffed. "Coming from you!"

We giggled at each other. There was something so easy about Hugo. It made me wonder why I had train wreck experiences with other boys.

"Alright," he said as our giggling tapered off. "Now as long as you wear clothes that fit you, I think we're good to go for Friday."

I swatted his shoulder and he laughed at his own joke impishly. "I'm serious, Ingrid. I'm really tired of seeing your butt cheeks all the time."

I flushed and fell back on his bed in a fit of laughter as he continued.

"A bra is never a bad idea! We can see your eyeliner from across the field! Ingrid, stop laughing! I'm being serious! Really!"

I continued to cackle, and it only made him laugh harder too. Soon we were two limp bodies, wheezing next to each other in what looked like a psychotic break.

"You're my best friend," I said breathily, grabbing his hand.

"And you're mine," he replied easily.

We rolled up to the bonfire in Corey's jeep. For some reason I imagined it would look like a Kesha music video, but the vibe was much more Mumford and Sons. One of the team's senior players was hosting, and the fire pit at his family's countryside home was the location.

When we popped open the doors of the jeep, our ears were assaulted with fuzzy house music blaring from someone's iPhone. There was something effortlessly cool about all of this. Hugo's team members were pulling up in cars beside us, girls with heavy eyeliner and denim shorts were being dragged by the hand to the fire pit, and someone was discreetly showing off a bottle of smuggled vodka he planned to dump in the punch later.

I buzzed with excitement. I never thought I'd be doing this again, but here we were—and this time I didn't have to spend my entire night trying to get my crush's attention. I already had it.

Corey rounded the jeep and laced his fingers with mine. "Let's go, Sunshine."

Hugo had been in the backseat of Corey's jeep, and he stood beside me now, rigid, holding his breath, and shrinking within himself like a turtle. I pulled the wrist of his hoodie to encourage him to follow us, which he did after a gulp and a slight stumble.

"You alright, Guerra?" Corey asked, glancing at Hugo with a pinch of concern I found endearing. "It's just the team, dude."

Hugo tried to smile reassuringly, but the dread in his eyes was unconvincing. As always, he looked like a cornered animal ready to accept death.

Corey squeezed my hand and leaned into my side to whisper, "Maybe some punch will help."

I snorted at the idea and glanced at Hugo. He seemed to get twitchier the closer we got. I wanted to reach out and grab his hand, but even I knew how that looked.

We came up to the fire pit and squeezed together on one of the benches, Hugo on one side, Corey on the other. Around us the other members of the team and their girlfriends stood around bobbing their heads to the music and talking excitedly. I drank it all in: the setting sun, the smell of smoke as the boy whose house this was started the bonfire, the passing of solo cups and punch. I wanted to squeal in delight. This is the scene I always wanted to be a part of.

Corey placed a hand on my thigh and pressed a kiss to my cheek. "Wanna grab some of the boozy punch and disappear for awhile?"

It was incredible how little I had to work to be desirable. Before I would spend bottomless hours throwing myself in front of a guy for him to barely glance at me. Now I felt all of their eyes on me, even the eyes of boys who had their hands in the back pockets of their girlfriend's denim shorts. And Corey. Corey wanted all my attention. It was thrilling and new. I couldn't get enough.

I nodded enthusiastically, and he stood to grab us some punch. As soon as he was gone I shifted toward Hugo and beamed, heart racing.

"Corey and I are going off alone for awhile," I told him, hoping he could see how happy I was and that he wouldn't try to ruin it.

"I heard," he said, bouncing his knees together. "Just don't be too long, okay? I'm allergic to this atmosphere and I won't hesitate to sprint home. I hate running, but I'll do it. I swear to you, Ingrid, I will."

Classic Depths of Despair Hugo. I snorted and bumped elbows with him. "I'd love to see you run."

He looked at me with complete and total conviction, the seriousness of maniac. "I'll do it, don't test me."

Corey returned with two solo cups that smelled more like alcohol than they did fruit punch and I followed him off into the pasture toward haybales I should have known he wasn't kidding about.

"I'm surprised he didn't follow us back here to watch while we make out," Corey joked, but it felt meanspirited, and I frowned at him.

"You didn't have to agree to drive us here. Hugo was always going to come," I reminded him. It was a conversation we had before when I told him Hugo had to come with me. He seemed annoyed and kept making these kinds of jokes. As much as I liked Corey, I didn't care for that.

"You've got to understand," he explained as we took a seat behind a haybale and stretched out toward the empty field and tall grass. "It's weird that you always have to be with him. You're with me, now."

I frowned at him and swirled my drink around in my cup. "Hugo and I have been friends since we were six. Our parents don't let us do anything without each other. He's not going to just disappear. It's not like that."

Corey downed half his drink and didn't look at me. I hated that.

"He's not a threat—"

"You don't see the way he looks at you."

The sun was nearly gone now, and the dark was cool and quiet. I swallowed hard, trying to make my skipping heart find it's rhythm again. I should be numb to those accusations by now. True love shouldn't distrust like this. I thought I should do something to make those doubts of his go away.

"I only see you," I said softly. He ground his teeth together and finished off the rest of his punch.

How could I see anyone else? Did I not look at him like he was what poetry was made of? Could he not tell I swooned over him? Why was everything always about Hugo with everyone? How many times did I have to explain myself?

I decided to chug my own drink the way Corey had, and tried not to grimace at the bitter taste of alcohol as I tossed the cup aside. I would worry about the consequences of that later. I was going to be bold, I decided, so I grabbed his chin and tilted it toward me.

"You're my prince," I told him seriously, and he looked as though he was going to laugh at that declaration, but I kissed him before he got the chance—because, yes, I realize I sounded insane and I needed to quickly cover it up.

Thankfully, he accepted the invitation, and responded by gripping the back of my head and pulling me deeper into the kiss. Corey liked that game, getting into little tiffs and making out to make up. At first it was a rush, a frantic oh no, and then we were kissing madly and trailing hickeys down each other's necks.

We stayed behind the haybales for awhile, kissing and laughing and talking until all of a sudden I felt a buzzing dizziness in the back of my head.

"Want to get more punch?" He asked breathlessly, his hand lingering at my waist beneath my t-shirt.

I nodded and stood, giggling at the way the world seemed weightless while I felt heavy and off-balance.

"I've never drank before," I whispered to him, like it wasn't completely obvious.

He grabbed our cups off the ground and threw an arm over my shoulder. "Oh, I know," he said with an amused grin. "You've only had a little and you're already buzzed."

We walked back to the fire pit where everyone else was bouncing about and laughing loudly. From a distance I recognized Hugo was sitting right where we left him, but he wasn't alone. Beside him a willowy, dark-haired girl sat in an oversized hoodie mirroring his bouncing knees and hunched shoulders. He smiled shyly at her for a moment and then turned toward Corey and I as though he could sense us coming.

"Looks like Hugo made a friend," Corey noted, observing me closely as he made the comment.

My eyes stuck on her for a moment, trying to place her. She looked familiar, but I didn't know how. "Wonder who she is."

"Hey," Hugo greeted us when we were close enough. The girl looked back and I recognized her, not because I knew her well, but because I'd seen her among our classmates. "This is Fiona. She's Wyatt's sister."

Wyatt, the host of tonight's bonfire. She was here because she lived here, not because she was dating anyone. My foggy brain processed that weird. Instead of feeling excited for

Hugo, I twisted to Corey and told him I was getting another drink. I realized I didn't really want to meet her.

I watched from the picnic table where I filled my cup with more spiked punch as Corey grinned between them. Fiona watched Hugo's every move and leaned into him the way I leaned into every boy I thought was going to be my prince. She seemed tall, athletic. Her hair was wild and curly. She looked funny, interesting. Someone I imagined Hugo would be intimidated by, but he looked unbothered.

I frowned and tapped my foot, deciding whether to go back or not. I really didn't want to. I'd rather just stay at this creepy distance and pretend I wasn't being insane. It had to be the alcohol.

Corey motioned for me to come over, and so I had to get the crazy look out my eye while I made my way. Not an easy task when every step feels clumsy and disorienting.

"Fiona was just telling me you two have something in common," Corey told me while pulling me into his side.

It was a truly calculated amount of curiosity I had to fake when I asked, "Really?"

"You both got sent to the principal's office for wearing off-the-shoulder shirts last year. Neat, huh?" He asked. He had the same fakeness in his voice. Maybe it was a side effect of the alcohol.

Who knew I'd be forced to bond with someone for exposing too much shoulder during 80's Day in the eighth grade? This was enough for me, I decided. I was good. No more.

"Cool," I said, distantly. "I thought I was the only one."

"I have to admit," Fiona said, her voice much richer than I was expecting. "I thought you and Hugo were a thing."

Great. Here we go again. Should I just walk into the fire and end it all?

"Everyone does," I said, taking a sip of my drink. It wasn't that special.

Hugo's eyebrows lifted at that, concerned. Sensing the hostile tone, he stood. Fiona's eyes saddened when his presence left her side.

Oh, please.

"Can I talk to her for a second?" He asked Corey.

"You've never needed my permission before," he replied. I ignored the way it sounded like an eyeroll.

Hugo paused, seeming to catch the loathing too. I thought he might say something in retort, but he wasn't one for confrontation. Instead he strode toward me and took me by the arm to lead me to a spot a couple feet away. His expression was hard to read, like a disgruntled babysitter who doesn't want the kids to know he's fed up.

"I think we should go," he said sternly.

"Why? Aren't you having fun with Fiona?" I asked. I meant to tease him, but it came out sour.

His head cocked to the side, and for a moment I thought I saw him smile. "Are you...jealous?"

I scoffed at him. "Come on, Hugo. Not you, too."

"Okay," he said. Simple as that, he dropped it.

I sipped at my drink and let my attention wander over to where Corey was. He and Fiona were sitting beside each other where we left them. I wanted to start all of that over. Corey was probably upset with me and Fiona probably thought I was a bitch. I didn't like it when people thought bad of me. It made my insides seize with regret and embarrassment. Everything was too blurry to take care of that now.

"I want to go home," I said.

Hugo nodded and pulled his phone out of his pocket to call his dad. The rest of the time we were there we hung out at the edge of the crowd not talking to each other. When his dad arrived, he didn't say anything about how I smelled like vodka or ask why we wanted to leave when we'd only been there two hours.

Corey told me we'd talk later about everything. I didn't know whether to be comforted or not. One thing I knew for sure: redemption was not my forte. Being perpetually embarrassing was, though.

Chapter 17

My first day of freshman year, I woke to a good morning text from Corey and a "be ready at 7:30" text from Hugo. After the party, Corey and I fought about Hugo in a long, dramatic series of texts that ended in me agreeing that Hugo wouldn't be a ride along to anymore dates.

He claimed I was too attached to Hugo. Honestly, though, it wasn't my fault Hugo and I were tied together at the wrist for all eternity. If he was going to blame anything, it should be the stars. That's just the way it was. But Corey wasn't having it.

I tried to keep Hugo oblivious to all of this. The last thing I needed right now was a know-it-all smirk disguised in a lecture. Besides, I was currently preoccupied with other matters.

When I hopped into the Guerra's red minivan that morning, Hugo smiled largely and settled back into his seat with a sigh of relief.

"Off to a good start, the tank tops are put to rest," he teased.

I rolled my eyes and tapped around my head to make sure my messy bun hadn't been messed up on the walk to the car. He watched with amusement, and I narrowed my eyes at him.

He was wearing one of his nicer shirts, and I had never seen those jeans before.

"You look nice," I commented suspiciously.

He shrugged and pretended to inspect his stubby nails.

His hair was even combed out of his face—and did I detect...cologne? I gasped.

"Did you dress up for high school?" Appalling, truly. Hugo?

"He insisted on new school clothes..." Mrs. Guerra noted, smirking over her shoulder as she pulled out of my driveway.

He sat up at that, cheeks rosy. "Nothing fit! I'm growing!"

Mrs. Guerra and I shared a look in the rearview mirror. I couldn't resist what I said next, she'd set me up perfectly for my latest attack.

"Or maybe he's trying to impress...I don't know...Fiona?"

"I've told you a hundred times, Ingrid. No!" He shrank back and shielded his face from his mother and I, his face turning blotchy. I swear I saw beads of sweat forming at his hairline. Bingo.

I giggled and prodded him. "Fiona," I sang.

Mrs. Guerra was chuckling to herself over this exchange. I think she was excited at the prospect of her cynical son having a normal teenage function.

I was more excited. Sure, he was being reluctant about admitting it, but cupid had finally stuck Hugo. I was certain. It was a miracle.

"Oh my god, Ingrid," Hugo groaned, lifting his shirt over his nose so we couldn't see his cheeks. What he didn't realize was that his whole face was beet red now. I released a hysteric cackle. "I will kill you," he muttered through his shirt.

I was at the point of obsession. Fiona. If I wasn't thinking about Corey, I was thinking about her. She was cute—and obviously nice because Hugo wouldn't have looked so comfortable next to her at the bonfire had she been a Stella. Hugo with Fiona. Fiona and Hugo. Cute.

I don't know why he tried to hide it. I was the last person he should be hiding it from.

"I talked to her for, like, fifteen minutes," he insisted, scowling at me.

"Hugo, I fall in love in fifteen seconds. Time means nothing to me," I told him, unconvinced. I wanted so badly for him to just tell me he liked her. I reached over to pull his shirt down from his face to unveil that telltale blush. He swatted me away and put a hand up in warning.

"Oh, you two are adorable," Mrs. Guerra sighed to herself.

Hugo continued to scowl while being curled awkwardly away from me in his seat. "She has no evidence," he whined pathetically. "I'm being framed."

We pulled into the school parking lot and I halted my teasing so I could get a good view of my new life. Hundreds of teenagers huddled outside the front door waiting to be let in. Everyone seemed so tall and old, I hardly felt qualified. Hugo suddenly appeared average height in comparison to our new peers.

The building was huge and sprawling. My stomach dropped at the thought of navigating it. My eyes searched desperately among the crowd for Corey. Josie. Anyone. The thrill of a new year never failed to fire me up. I glanced back at Hugo who looked out with indifference—or maybe silent fear. I could hardly tell these days.

"Alright you two, I'll see you at the game tonight." Mrs. Guerra turned to look at us, eyes softening and her smile tightening like she was trying hard to hold back tears. "Wasn't that long ago I was here with Maria." She shook her head, blinking quickly. "Stop growing!"

I sat forward and pressed my cheek to hers in goodbye. Hugo allowed her to press a wet, lipstick kiss to his cheek, which I immediately helped him rub it away before we exited the car. One hundred "I love you's" later, and we tumbled out to join our classmates among the flag pole.

I noticed Hugo scanning the crowd, craning his neck instead of shrinking away. My eyebrows lifted at that.

"Searching for Fiona?"

He sighed deeply, his shoulders dropping as he looked down at me. "You don't really think I like her, do you?" He asked, his voice serious.

I scoffed. "Oh, c'mon. You totally do. You can tell me."

He frowned. "You're being weird about this."

"What are you talking about?" I asked, rolling forward onto my toes, heart fluttering. "I'm happy for you. I just wish you'd tell me."

He looked at me strangely, like he did at the bonfire. Head slightly cocked, a smile so small you might miss it. My buzzed brain remembered that look. It made my heart pound, feel almost guilty.

I shoved that feeling down and turned away in time to see Josie break out of the crowd and skip toward us with a giant grin plastered across her metal free mouth. "Hey, lovebirds, what did you do with your summers? Finally make-out in the back row of The Cosmo?"

I rolled my eyes but let her grip me in a side-hug. "No." I released her with a gentle shove. "I'm dating a junior on the soccer team, thank you very much. Hugo, on the other hand, joined said soccer team and is very much in love with Fiona Carlton."

"Holy shit. What?" She looked between us in disbelief. "We don't see each other for three months and you do all the fun stuff without telling me?"

Hugo sent me a look of complete exhaustion and crossed his arms. "I'd just like to point out that I am not in love with Fiona."

Josie wrinkled her nose. "Denial has never been a look on you, Hugo."

Hugo's arms tightened in stubborn rejection, teeth gritting slightly. "Not denial. I really don't like Fiona. Ingrid, why?"

I was too busy looking out among our classmates, searching for our final crew member to answer his question. "Where's Micah?" I asked Josie.

She pointed somewhere off in the distance and flicked back a few of her curls. "With his boyfriend up at the front. For the record, I'm single. Thanks for asking."

I waggled my eyebrows at her. "Come to a soccer game with me and you won't be."

"I don't want to be a part of this conversation anymore," Hugo interjected. The amount of done in his eyes had to be record-breaking. I thought he might storm away, but he didn't have anywhere to run.

Josie and I giggled, interrupted only by the opening of the school doors.

Corey found me among the chaos at the freshman locker bay before homeroom. He'd done the first day of high school already, none of this fazed him.

I shrieked and swiveled into my locker door when he pinched my sides to get my attention. "Hey, Sunshine. How's the first day so far?"

My face flushed, and I steadied the locker door. He was supposed to find me leaning against a wall somewhere, with a full pout and effortless grace. But, of course, nothing went my way.

Rubbing my sore shoulder, I put on my most seductive smile and batted my lashes. "Perfect now," I said sweetly, hoping I didn't look as frazzled as I felt.

He grinned at the effort and placed his hands on my waist, pulling me close. "I've got something for you. All our girls wear these at our games."

In my shocked state, I hadn't noticed he had anything with him. Then, my eyes locked on a white stretch of fabric hanging over his shoulder. He pulled it off and held it up to my chest. I bounced in excitement when I realized what it was.

"We make 'em for you. That's my number, twenty-four."

I looked down at the paint splatter shirt, blue and green like our school colors. A giant number '24' was written smack dab in the middle. I bit my lip to stop the excitement from bubbling out. We were so official as a couple. My heart swelled.

I loved him.

He watched my reaction in adoration and then tilted my chin up to kiss me.

My life was a dream, a high school movie. Name a more perfect boyfriend? Impossible. He was mine.

He pulled back and smiled down at me, rubbing his thumbs against my cheeks. "Let me walk you to homeroom," he proposed.

A sinking feeling swept over me. He wasn't going to like what I was going to say, and he seemed to read my mind as soon as the excited flurries vanished from my eyes.

He dropped his hands from my face. "Are you kidding?"

"I promised. Hugo and I stick together on the first day. We're each other's safety blanket," I tried to explain.

Corey rolled his eyes and stepped back. "I'm sure he can manage. He's grown. No more safety blanket."

I shook my head, frowning. Was it naïve of me to want to believe that eventually Corey would accept Hugo as an extension of myself? Would he do whatever he could to butt Hugo out for good? I bit the inside of my cheeks at the thought. Corey was my one. I wasn't going to give up on him.

Hugo approached us cautiously, seeming to sense some tension. I locked eyes with him and shook my head. His eyes flitted between us, trying to guess what was wrong. Corey noticed and glanced over his shoulder, groaning when he saw Hugo.

"Fine," he said, throwing his arms up. "It's fine. I guess I'll just schedule when I get to be alone my girlfriend."

"Corey—"

He strode off without looking back, disappearing around the corner back to the junior bay. I stared after him helplessly and fell back against my locker door, shutting it with a short clang.

Great. Could I have a drama free romance just once?

Hugo took a step forward, eyebrows stitched together. "What was that about?"

What was I supposed to say? Corey hates you?

One argument at a time. That was not a can of worms I needed to open.

Thankfully, Josie cut off any further discussion by bounding toward us with reckless abandon, squealing, "Oh my god, he is such a babe."

Now this. This was a conversation I could get on board with.

Hugo snorted. "Should have seen the booty shorts she wore to get his attention."

Josie turned to me accusingly, "Wait, I thought you were against that?"

I rolled off the lockers with a sigh. "These are not gross boys, Josie," I told her. "These are guys. They don't just sit around making jokes, they actually make moves. It's totally different now."

She made a point of looking square at Hugo when she said, "Whatever you say."

He didn't acknowledge her little stare-down, and instead motioned toward the clock. "Let's get to homeroom."

The soccer game was supposed to be the highlight of my day. What more could a girl ask for? A sweaty, rugged half-man playing for her affection in the glow of a setting sun? Check. Achievement complete.

I got settled onto the aluminum bleachers I spent all summer lounging on. We'd ended the school day with a pep rally, and boy was I filled with pep. Josie and I had just finished getting ready for the game in the girls bathroom. We both sported green and blue eye shadow, but only I wore the enviable paint splattered t-shirt that meant I belonged to a guy on our team.

Josie pointed toward our team, warming up on the left half of the field. Their opponents were just now filing off the bus. "Look, there's your man."

I brightened at that. Ah, what a lovely phrase that was. My man. Corey was in better spirits now. He'd even given me a passionate kiss when he saw me in the t-shirt that marked me as his.

He must have realized he was being talked about and turned toward us after making a practice goal. With a wink, he blew me a kiss. He seemed satisfied to see me sitting with Josie instead of some other secret boyfriend I might have.

"You're so lucky," Josie whined. "You, Micah, possibly Hugo. How dare you all leave me single. I mean, really, Hugo."

"Unconfirmed," I told her. "Just a suspicion. Oh, there she is. Fiona."

That wild-haired, bronze beauty climbed the bleachers, throwing looks over her shoulder toward our team. Fiona. I could feel her lust for Hugo from where I was sitting. Who else would she be looking at?

Josie giggled and scoped her out. Like me, she eyeballed her as she took a seat with her family a few seats away. Then she was waving.

I looked to see who at and began to twist my fingers together when I realized it was Hugo who waved back.

Josie's brows hiked up. "Confirmed."

Slut.

I frowned at myself and pinched my fingers together.

"You good?"

I glanced sideways at Josie, who was making a face at my twisted fingers.

"Uh—"

Thunk.

A soccer ball bounced off Hugo's head and went sailing across the field. I made to stand but Josie placed a hand on my shoulder. "He's good."

Corey ran toward him. "Sorry, dude!"

Hugo rubbed the side of his head and put a hand out to stop Corey from coming any closer. My heart shouldn't have been racing while some unknown dialogue passed between them, but a nervous pit settled in my stomach anyway.

"Is it wrong of me to want to see them brawl?" Josie wondered out loud, her voice swaying towards laughter.

I nudged her. "That's the last thing I want."

She bit back a mischievous grin.

The Guerra's joined Josie and I at the top of the bleachers and cheered for Hugo the whole game even though he stepped onto the field a grand total of zero times. Corey, on the other hand, was the reason our school won. Every goal meant a kiss blown in my direction. The Guerra's found that absolutely endearing. I spent the whole game daydreaming Corey was in a battle for my heart. He won in a landslide. Not a soldier on the field remained.

We stormed the field after the win, and I jumped into Corey's arms in a victorious display of PDA. He stank of grass and sweat, and he kissed me with vigor. It was like being embraced by a grizzly hero.

"What do I get for winning?" He panted against my lips.

"Whatever you want," I said, blushing.

He set me down and tucked a loose hair behind my ear. "I'll remember that."

Hugo and Josie were talking to his parents. She waved to me as she pulled away and backed toward the parking lot.

"I gotta go! See you tomorrow!"

"See ya!"

Corey watched her walk away. "Hugo's girl?"

I shook my head. "Nope, just a friend."

I guess he was hopeful, because his smile drooped. As for myself, I quickly searched the field for Fiona, smiling to myself when I saw her leaving with her family. I kissed his cheek. "The Guerra's are my ride."

He kissed me hard before we parted ways. Hugo's parents had already started making their way toward the van.

I met Hugo at the bleachers where he was collecting his things. He pushed back his sweaty hair and threw the strap of his bag over his shoulder.

We walked to the van together, but I noticed his chest seemed tight, his posture slightly rigid like it gets when he's working up the will to say something. Finally, after a few paces, he glanced over to my boyfriend's jeep and said, "Corey doesn't like me, huh?"

I followed Hugo's gaze and allowed a few steps to pass, thinking about Corey. I didn't want Hugo to know about any of the ugly stuff.

"He likes you." It sounded like a lie.

Hugo snorted. He was a better people reader than I was. "If he thinks you're watching me instead of him, he lashes out."

"No, he doesn't," I said, but I was watching my feet now. I admit, I didn't think Hugo getting a ball kicked at his head was an accident.

He stopped and grabbed my wrist to stop me too. A few of his teammates passed alongside us, and he waited for them to get out of hearing distance. I looked toward the Guerra minivan and shuffled uncomfortably.

"I don't think you should come to practice anymore," he suggested carefully, his voice soft. "I guess you have to come to the games, but at least I'm benched for most of it."

I looked at him in disbelief at what he was suggesting. "It's not like that."

But who was I trying to convince? Myself?

"It is, though, Ingrid."

He didn't understand how complicated Corey could be. I knew he didn't want Hugo in the picture. Period. I knew that eventually he was going to want me to choose. I just needed time. I could still change the course of this relationship. I could make everything work. I could have everything. He was the one, everything had to be fine.

Nevertheless, Hugo's conviction was scaring me, so I began to walk away. They always said love is blind.

Chapter 18

"Come sit with me," Corey suggested, ducking down to rest his chin on my shoulder.

I sat with Hugo and Josie at a small round table in the cafeteria. It was late September and Micah was still off galivanting with his boyfriend's friend group, leaving Josie in awkward limbo. If she wasn't wailing about being a third wheel, she was pouting about being without a boyfriend herself. If Corey had things his way, Josie and Hugo would be new best friends and I, like Micah, would disappear.

I'd already turned down the offer several times before, but it was only creating fights. I glanced at Hugo, whose eyes immediately fell to his tray. He nodded subtly and pretended to be really interested in his green beans. Josie's eyes grew with anticipation. She never understood how I could refuse.

I took a deep breath and stood. With a victorious whoop, Corey pulled me in close and pressed a kiss to my cheek.

"Finally!"

"Have fun, Ingrid!" Josie sang while I lifted my lunch tray and turned to follow Corey.

Hugo gave me his best fake smile, but his posture didn't curl in on itself like I expected it too. He remained neutral and shifted himself towards Josie. That was the only thing making me okay with leaving. At least he wasn't completely alone. Just two half-friends pretending they weren't being totally betrayed by their besties.

"I think you guys could be friends," I tried to convince Hugo last Saturday afternoon behind the register at The Bread Basket.

I sat atop the counter behind him sorting jelly packets, swinging my feet nervously.

He turned and watched me for a moment without saying anything, and then he shrugged.

"Yeah, he was really nice to me before you guys started going out. And then you did, and I became a threat, so..." He crossed his arms and met my gaze. "I'm pleasant with him. He's the one with the issue, Ingrid. I'm sorry."

I squished a strawberry jelly packet between my fingers and sighed. "Are you sure?"

Hugo rolled his eyes and turned back around. "You know, maybe I should hang out with Josie or Fiona or whatever. Some girl who isn't you."

I scowled and threw the jelly into the box. "What's that supposed to mean?"

"I don't know." He gripped the counter top with both hands and looked out across the room. I frowned deeply at him, my heart quickening with anger at the suggestion. "Maybe I wouldn't get tripped every day at practice," he said.

I blinked several times at that admission. "You said things were better."

"I've been saying a lot of things."

I gritted my teeth at the amount of attitude oozing from him. It wasn't normal. Just like with Corey, Hugo and I seemed to be constantly fighting our way through rough patch after rough patch.

"Look," I explained. "I've been trying not to prioritize him over you. I thought I was doing the right thing."

He shook his head and looked over his shoulder. "For my sake, please just put him first," he told me softly.

"This is Ingrid," Corey's voice rang in my ear, and I looked out at the group of people in front of me with a tense smile. Corey introduced me to them.

Only one other girl, Cheyanna, sat there with her boyfriend. I sunk down between her and Corey. When she threw her straight black hair over her shoulder, it brushed my arm.

"So," she said, leaning back to get a better look at me. "You're a freshman?"

I nodded. The part of me that would normally be doing backflips at the chance to hang out with upperclassmen and pretend I was cool enough to be one of them was crying out helplessly from it's cage. Instead I felt like I was sleepwalking, completely disconnected.

Corey seemed to notice and threw an arm over my shoulder. "Cute, right?"

"What, did you finally work your way through the sophomore class? Fresh meat?" His large friend, Adam, joked. They all giggled at that, and I flushed.

"Girls don't like hearing their boyfriend is a total whore," Cheyanna chastised with a roll of her eyes. She put her hand on mine and reassured me, "His last relationship was exactly three weeks long, so you're setting new records. Maybe you're the one."

"The one that's not putting out," her boyfriend blurted out with sharp cackle.

She shoved him. "You're all disgusting. She's a baby."

"Trust me, if she's with Corey, she won't be for long."

They all whooped and hollered over that, but I was shrinking and burning red as a tomato. It was almost worse than sitting in the living room with my mom getting the talk. This isn't what I talked about with my friends.

"Hey, hey, hey, hey, hey!" Corey shouted overtop of them, shaking his head. "It's not like that."

"Yeah, okay..."

"Oh, shut up," Cheyanna said. "Stop harassing the poor girl."

Corey nodded. "Thank you, Chey."

I leaned in close to him and whispered, "Can I go sit with my friends now?"

He laughed a little and rubbed my shoulder. "They're just teasing. Stay with me."

And, well, Corey was my first priority now, so I couldn't argue with that.

Hugo and I sat across from each other doing homework on his bed. He smelled like soap from his after-practice shower and every few seconds a bead of water would slide off a strand of his hair onto his textbook, but he was too focused to care.

I tapped my pencil against my notebook and watched for a couple minutes, trying to get up the nerve to bring up something very off topic. I felt weird all day after lunch with Corey, and I just couldn't shake it.

Drip, drip, drip.

I took a breath and got up, tiptoeing lightly across the room to very gently shut the door—which was absolutely not allowed.

Hugo looked up at me and then glanced at the door.

"Uhh—?"

I tiptoed back across the room and sat down. Unable to look at him directly, I pinched my fingers together and watched my knuckles turn white.

"Do you..." I took a deep breath. "Do you think we should be talking about sex?"

"Umm..." He set his pencil down in the crease of his book and went still. "I don't know...?"

"It's just my mom brought it up a little while ago, and that's all Corey's friends kept wanting to talk about it...and I think Corey's had a lot of sex." I bit my lip and slowly looked up to try and meet his eye.

The idea that Corey had a lot of sex was the most uncomfortable for me. I suddenly felt a lot of pressure to drown my innocence. I was embarrassed by how embarrassed I was.

He looked at me strangely, and seemed to be trying very hard to not blush, but his neck clearly wasn't following orders. "Ingrid I've never even kissed anyone. I don't have a reason to talk about it."

"But, do you, like, ever think about it?"

"God, Ingrid!" He pushed his books off his lap and propped his elbows up on his knees instead, burying his face in his hands. "I don't—ugh, I...Are you? Are you thinking about doing it?" His voice sounded strained.

I shrugged helplessly. All knowledgeable Hugo was supposed to be helpful, here.

"Should I be?"

He scoffed and dragged his fingers down his face. "Do you want to?"

"I don't think so..." I paused. "I mean, I've thought about it—"

He scooted way far back at that admittance and put his hands up. "Okay, okay, no. That's too much for me."

I narrowed my eyes at him and stood. "What? Too grown up for you? Who else am I going to talk to?"

"Josie?" He suggested without hesitation.

"But you're my best friend!"

He scoffed again and rolled his eyes. "On the days Corey can't hang out."

"You told me to make him a priority," I said defensively.

"I know."

"Then don't get mad when I do!"

He stood up then, towering over me. "Well it's not like I want things that way." I glared up at him. "Look Ingrid," he said, lowering his voice and glancing quickly at the door and then back at me. "I'm sorry, but I don't want to know what you do with him. Have sex with him or don't. But I don't want to know about it. I thought I did but I don't. It's gotten to the point where I don't."

I threw my arms up in exasperation. "You said not to shut you out, but now you're shutting me out. Make up your mind, Hugo. This isn't easy for me!"

"Shouldn't it be easy, though?" He asked, frustrated. "Easier than this?"

"I'm working on it, Hugo."

"Fine," he snapped.

"Fine."

We stood glaring at each other. Waiting for the other to concede. It felt oddly charged. Like even though we'd just vented, each of us was still holding something back. Maybe it was the sex talk or a thousand romantic comedies stored up in my brain, but it almost felt tense. The kind of tense that occurs right before someone goes for it. But the guilt seeped in and I broke off the heated eye contact to push the hair out of my face. Hugo sat and pulled his book back into his lap.

"Open the door. Someone might think we're having sex in here," Hugo gritted out with a touch more sarcasm than I'm used to.

The weird moment disappeared and the bitterness overflowed. "Right. You've never even kissed anyone."

He glowered at me. "You don't have to stay, you know? If you're going to be a jerk, you can go home."

I crossed the room and pulled the door open dramatically. "I thought you didn't care about that stuff. How can I be a jerk if you don't care?"

"Don't act like it wasn't supposed to be hurtful," he said lowly. "You know what you meant."

"Fine, I'm sorry. I'm sorry, okay? Just forget about all of it. I'm sorry I brought it up." I sat back down across from him and pulled my homework into my lap, as well.

He watched me get settled, his face still red and sunken into a scowl. I looked back at him and bit my cheek.

"I'm not going to have sex with him, for the record," I said quietly.

His eyes flicked downwards and he twirled his pencil between his fingers. "Okay."

A couple minutes passed in silence, and then Hugo turned his page and decided to break the barrier. "For the record," he said. "I know I've led you to think I'm above it, but I'm not. I do want to be with someone someday, and I'm still waiting for the right time to kiss her. That's all you need to know. Since we're talking about uncomfortable things."

I smiled down at my notebook and resisted the urge to leap over and hug him, but I'd known Hugo so long that I knew he'd rather I pretend I never heard it. So, I finished writing a sentence and turned the page of my notebook without acknowledgement.

The grinch did have a heart, after all.

Chapter 19

After Hugo's little confession I thought I'd be seeing Fiona a lot more, but alas, she remained a side character. Sometimes I'd see them talking at his locker, sometimes she'd sit with Hugo and Josie during lunch for a few minutes before trotting back over to sit with her friends. It was a truly confusing phenomenon. He was talking about Fiona, right?

I was trying not to be so weird about it. I had no reason to be weird about it. I had Corey. Hugo need someone too. And since Corey was doing everything in his power to make sure I spent as little time with Hugo as possible, it was no longer my business. So, for the first time, all I could do was sit back and watch.

No, really.

Corey was now driving me to school most days, which was enough fuel for my mother's fire. Her and her boyfriend always had something embarrassing to say to me on my way out the door. Some days I'd walk out to some tragic soliloquy about how I was growing up too fast.

Hugo didn't really talk about it. He said his piece and now it was radio silence. Josie didn't help. First she was on my side, but now she was entirely convinced that if anything it was one-sided, and Hugo wasn't the one trying to make moves.

If I seemed a little fixated with the whole thing, it's because I was. It had been a long time since I'd spent time with my friends. I felt suspended and so far from everything. All I had was Corey. Corey and his stupid, vulgar friends.

I was homesick.

"Did you get your dress for homecoming?" Corey asked me on a particularly depressing Wednesday afternoon in October.

I lifted books out of my backpack and started exchanging them for the ones I'd need for my afternoon courses.

"No," I said flatly.

"Homecoming is Friday, why don't you have your dress?" He asked, blocking me off from my locker so I had to look at him.

I restrained myself from swatting him away, because he hated that. "I don't know. I thought I'd skip the game tonight and go shopping with Josie or something."

"Were you going to tell me you weren't coming to the game?" He asked, a little more emotional than I was in the mood to deal with.

"I was getting to it."

"When?"

I bit back a smart reply and just said, "Later."

He stared at me in disbelief. "You have to come to the game. You love coming to the games. You can go shopping tomorrow, I guess."

Well, I used to love coming to the games. Now it was just a chore. Making sure I was one-hundred-percent focused on just him, cheering loud enough that he could hear me specifically, getting a ride home with him after a victory make-out. I wasn't one to say romance was dead—but the romance was dead.

He was the one, so I was hanging onto hope that our twirling music box of love was going to be reset soon. The tune was warped, the ballerina was teetering forward at snail pace, and just being around the choppy melody was giving me a headache. Most days my heart felt like it was going to implode.

"Fine," I said, because there's no arguing with Corey.

"Good." He gave me a short kiss and stepped out of my way. "So, who's Hugo going with? I'm surprised you don't want him tagging along."

My eyes fell shut, and I heaved in a giant breath. The ticking time bomb in my heart burst.

"Why are you so obsessed with him?" I snapped, turning quickly on him with a dagger-like stare, hands clenched in fists.

"What?"

"Yeah, you're being obsessive." I shoved my final textbook in my bag and zipped it shut. "I hardly talk to Hugo anymore, Corey. Stop asking questions about him."

He slammed my locker shut for me and grabbed onto my elbow to stop me from walking away from him. "You see him every week, you have dinner with his family. Don't act like I never let you see him."

I pulled out of his grasp in one swift motion and took a few steps away. "Ah, the one thing you can't take away from me." I narrowed my eyes at him and marched off, feeling the heat of the explosion wash over me. "Well he'd rather ignore me these days instead of getting bullied by you at practice, so actually, I have no idea anymore. Stop bringing him up. It's exhausting."

"You're being a little dramatic, Ingrid," he told me, following a step behind me while I made my way to class.

I bit my lip, eyes watering a little. Maybe I was. I'd stopped doodling mine and Corey's name in hearts. I stopped looking at him with adoration. I stopped getting excited to see him. Maybe there was something wrong with me. This wasn't me. I'd become someone else. I felt a thousand miles away. I just wanted to go back to being me.

I was supposed to be in love. I loved love.

"Fine," I said, stopping in front of my classroom. I let the rage dissipate and embarrassment take its place. "I'll see you at the game. You're right, I'm being dramatic."

He beamed like the fight wasn't real. "That's a good girl." He pressed a kiss to my forehead. "I'll see you later, Sunshine."

I didn't even watch him walk away. I just stepped into class tiredly. Hugo stared curiously at me from his desk.

I sat in my assigned seat in front of him and he reached out to tap my shoulder.

"You okay?"

I smiled tightly, knowing my eyes were glassy and unconvincing. "All constellations and rainbows."

He shook his head gently, eyes flitting between mine with concern, "No it's not."

"No it's not," I repeated in a whisper, brushing away a spilled tear.

"Do you want to come over after the game? We can watch one of those horrible movies you like," he suggested with a half-grin.

I mirrored his grin but shook my head. "Corey."

Hugo nodded and sat back. "Right."

The unflattering lights in the department store certainly weren't doing me any favors as I held up a dress in front of me and inspected it in a mirror.

"How about this one?"

My mom peeked up from one of the racks she was browsing through and gave me a thumbs up.

"That one's pretty."

"You don't think I'll look like a marshmallow?" I asked skeptically, swaying the bouncy fabric from side to side in front of me.

She shrugged. "Looks like a variation of something I wore in the eighties."

"Alright, so that's a no..." I muttered to myself, sticking the dress back on the rack.

It was my own fault for waiting this long to go dress shopping. I just wasn't that excited to do it.

"You seem a little down, Ingrid," my mom said, as she weaved through the racks with an arm full of dresses. "Are you nervous?"

"No." It was my kneejerk reaction answer, unfortunately. I released a heavy sigh and stepped back from the dresses. "How'd you know it was time to get a divorce?"

She chuckled to herself. "Boy problems?"

I just crossed my arms over my chest and shrugged.

She nodded and twisted in place, thinking.

"Well, you know your father was my prince charming. I always thought that. Then he cheated and broke my heart. I was going to try to make it work but..." She sighed. "I couldn't even look at him anymore. Everything was a fight. He tried to make me feel like I was overreacting about everything—like I was the crazy one. We just fell out of love, I think."

I took a step back toward the rack and pushed some hangers aside, not really paying attention to the dress attached to them.

"Corey hates Hugo. A lot," I explained. "So, Hugo and I haven't really been hanging out anymore. But when I'm with Corey I just feel annoyed most of the time. It didn't used to be like that."

"Have you talked to him about it? Corey?"

I wanted to laugh at that. "He doesn't let me tell him anything. If he doesn't agree then it doesn't matter," I told her. And, wow, saying it out loud, it sounded bad.

"I don't like that," she said, her voice serious. "I think you should consider giving your relationship a reality check. If it's miserable and you hate being with him, why stay at all?"

I threw another dress selection over her arm and turned back to the rack, eyes downcast. "I like having a boyfriend," I mumbled.

She snorted and ran a hand through the ends of my hair, twirling little ringlets around her fingers. "Oh, sweetie. That's going to get you in trouble someday."

I gave her a sidelong glance and chewed the inside of my cheek for a moment, trying to think of some sort of justification for what I was doing with Corey. I wasn't one to just walk away from my one. Love was supposed to conquer all. But if my mother, the queen of all things Hollywood romance, was telling me things weren't looking good, then I couldn't ignore the bad stuff anymore. Corey was getting one last chance, and that was that.

"Do you want to try these on?" She asked, lifting her dress laden arm into view.

I nodded, and she followed me to the dressing room to help me hang them on the door and then stepped out once I was settled.

"So," she started while I shimmied out of my sweater and jeans. I could see her feet under the door and watched her pace a few times. My brows furrowed at that, and I quickly unhooked the first dress from the hanger and pulled it up over my hips. "You know Pete and I have been dating for awhile now."

I rolled my eyes at that, because I'd lost count of what number man she was on a little while ago. But, yes, Man-Number-Whatever had been around for most of the year. He was alright. He liked to call me Grid and make me really sweet cups of coffee in the morning after he stayed the night.

"Sure," I said, pulling the zipper closed. I turned in the mirror, already hating how tight the aqua blue dress was. It was also a little short. I opened the door anyway to show her.

She made a face and shook her head when she saw it but put a hand on my shoulder to stop me from disappearing back into the dressing room. "We've been talking about the possibility of getting married."

I froze. "M-married? You? Married?"

A smile slowly spread across her face, and she nodded, cheeks turning rosy. "Possibly."

"What? When?" I pulled her hand off my shoulder and examined her fingers, dropping it in confusion. "Where's the ring?"

"Ingrid." She laughed a little and shook her head. "He didn't propose. We've just been talking about it. I want to see how you feel about the idea of Pete staying with us. Maybe he'll move in."

I stared blankly. "Moving in? When?"

What was going on? Where was this coming from?

"Only if you're comfortable with it," she added quickly.

"Well, he stays over so much that it already feels like he lives with us," I told her truthfully, mind spinning.

She really found her one? My mom always felt perpetually single to me. She was the break-up expert. What was I supposed to do with her now? Who was going to watch Bridget Jones's Diary with me for the twelfth time?

"So, you're okay with him moving in?" She asked hesitantly. She was watching me carefully. To be fair, I'd never been in this situation before. She probably thought I was going to have a meltdown. I really didn't give a crap about any of the men she dated, but now this one was staying.

"I don't know," I admitted. There was so much to unpack, here. I couldn't give her a solid answer. She had to know that. "Married, Mom?"

"Not yet. In the future," she assured me.

"You really found your one?"

Her smile widened, and I saw the same giddy look in her face that I saw in mine every time I fell for my new prince. "I really found him."

"Are you sure?" I asked, suddenly critical—and okay, maybe projecting a little. "Because I thought I found my one like ten times, and then it turned out I was wrong...every time."

She rubbed my shoulder gently. I'd never seen someone so twitterpatted in my life—except maybe me.

"Well, honey, he's become my best friend. We've been coworkers for years. We always got along. I was going out with random blind dates before, and we just didn't have that connection. Pete and I already had a foundation, and it just keeps getting better now." She spoke her truth into the air, as if directing it to God or Aphrodite or Cupid. It was just bursting from her, and I wondered why she never said anything before. "I really love him."

I searched her eyes and she nodded reassuringly. She was so confident, so in love and I hadn't even been paying at-tention. There was a new happy twinkle in her eye, a glow about her that was undeniable. I'd never seen her like this. My heart hurt at that revelation. Now I wasn't so sure I even knew what love was. Her love seemed deeper than any love I'd ever known.

"Okay," was all I said.

"Alright," she said, squeezing my shoulder. "Go try on those other dresses. This one is no good."

And that's how I found out I might be getting a new dad—oh, and that I have no clue what I'm doing with my love life. But no biggie.

Chapter 20

No one tells you that high school dances are just like middle school dances. Well, except for the grinding, and the sneaking in alcohol, and the police officer chilling at the entryway. Other than that, though, it's freaky familiar. Like, almost disturbingly familiar.

I'd never attended a dance with a date before so that was new, I guess. I was on edge, though. Maybe it was the shot Corey insisted we did in his jeep before walking through the doors, maybe it was the fact that he had room for one more mistake and didn't even know it, but I just had the worst feeling. And I always thought my first high school dance was going to be magical. So just imagine my disappointment.

"This dress fits you just right," Corey whispered in my ear as he pulled me in close by the waist at the coat drop-off.

I flashed him one of those dazzling smiles I'd perfected over the summer. What? He wasn't wrong. It's not like I wanted to break up. I truly wanted this to work. So if the dance went well, maybe we could stay together. So far things were going fine. It'd been almost an entire day and I hadn't wanted to pull my hair out, yet.

"Stunning," he had told me as I walked into the living room to meet him. He brought me a single red rose—which made my mother's brows twitch together. "Let's see all of it, Sunshine."

I spun on the toes of a pair of sparkly silver heels I could barely walk in to let him see the plunging back of my navy minidress. I even tossed my blonde curls about, making sure he noticed how bouncy they were. I had spent an hour in heavy, burning hot rollers after all.

He stood and opened his arms for me. "Not bad for a last-minute dress."

I closed the gap and pressed a kiss to his cheek.

"Alright, alright," my mom fussed. "Let me get a picture of you before you go."

She snapped a couple of photos but didn't seem too particularly interested in them—or Corey, actually. Maybe telling her all that stuff the night before wasn't the best idea. I could have waited until after the dance, you know, instead of before when they had to sit in the living room together and make small talk while I finished my makeup.

My mom was no stranger to faking nice, but she wasn't pulling off the best charade this time. She was hardly looking at him.

"Home before ten-thirty, please. Don't be late. I love you," she told me, ignoring Corey completely as she walked us to the door.

"I'll get her home safe and sound," Corey assured her with a brilliant movie star grin.

"Great," she said dismissively. "Be good."

We rounded the corner and entered the gymnasium which was already quaking with loud pop music. Some students surrounded the DJ and were swaying and bopping along to the beat. Green and blue balloons looked to be kicked aside to make more room for a dance floor.

My eyes scanned the crowd for Hugo or Josie or even Micah, but I couldn't make them out if they were there. Heck, I didn't even know if Hugo was coming. I wished I would have just texted him about it.

"I see Adam over there, let's go," Corey said, dragging me by the hand to follow him. I had to bite my tongue at that. There was no part of me that wanted to hang out with his friends.

But I was trying, really trying to make this work. And if it was going to work, I didn't need to be starting fights.

One bro handshake later, and we were pulled onto the dancefloor. I had never grinded with anyone in my life. The most sexual thing I'd ever done was make out with Corey behind a haybale a couple of months ago. And before that? I wore booty shorts and heavy eyeliner to boys soccer practice. Did I sometimes dance provocatively to Miley Cyrus Can't Be Tamed in the bathroom mirror? Sure, but who knows if I was even doing that right.

When Corey grabbed me by the waist and pressed his junk against my trunk, I nearly jumped out of my skin.

What the hell was that?

Corey laughed at that. "Just relax and rock with me."

Whatever that meant. So, I channeled my inner Britney Spears and went for it. Corey's hands hugged me in close and pressed his nose into my hair while we swayed together to some classic 2011 pop.

"Careful, Mrs. Edwards won't hesitate to pull you two apart," Cheyanna warned us while she eyeballed the teacher chaperones all whispering together in the corner. She and her boyfriend were bouncing a good distance apart, playing it surprisingly safe.

I glanced over in Mrs. Edwards direction, suddenly worried and self-conscious. As I did, I caught Hugo entering the gym with combed back hair and dress clothes. He looked a little unsettled, as always, eyes flitting about in search of someone he knew.

Then his eyes caught mine.

And of course, Cory was still swinging his hips into me.

Hugo looked away awkwardly and went to sit on the bleachers. It didn't matter that Hugo and I really weren't talking these days. That was my best friend sitting alone at his first high school dance. I couldn't believe he even decided to come.

Protective and homesick, I instinctively took a step toward him. How could I not?

Corey grabbed my hand and pulled me back. "Hey, I think I left my wallet in my car. I'm going to go grab it. Come with me." It was an order disguised as a suggestion, and he scanned my face quickly as he said it, searching for the softness and longing in my eyes that was apparently reserved only for Hugo.

I knew that fight. He liked that fight.

"Okay, let's go."

He led me off the dance floor and purposely around the side of the gym where Hugo wasn't hiding on the bleachers. I craned over all the jumping, dancing bodies trying to get a glimpse of him, but Corey rushed me out the door before I could look over my shoulder and make sure he was okay.

We stopped to collect our jackets and shoes and then he was guiding me out the front door toward his jeep. The air was brisk, and I pulled my jacket tightly over my chest. I didn't even bother with my shoes. I could barely walk in them, and it was too chilly to do anything but jog through the parking lot.

"I'm freezing," I whined.

"Maybe we can warm up in the jeep before we go back in," Corey said with a sly smile. I admit, a month ago I would have melted at that. I would have lost my mind and thrown myself at him like a lovesick fool. But he treated Hugo like a disease again, and it pulled me right out of the fantasy.

Each breath I released swirled into the wind like smoke. I had to jog in place just to stay warm while he unlocked the jeep. Five painful seconds later and I flung myself into the slightly warmer interior.

"Did I really have to come?" I moaned, shivering.

Corey started his car and turned the heat up. He was smiling one of his naughty smiles, and his bright blue eyes locked with mine as he pulled his wallet out of his pocket.

"Of course. I wanted my alone time," he said, leaning over the console to grasp the back of my neck. "And you look so good."

He pressed his lips to mine fervidly and let his hand tangle in my perfectly undone curls. There was no denying he was a great kisser, soft yet passionate—and an absolute master of the French kiss. If he thought he could momentarily distract me from my mixed feelings for him, he was absolutely right. He knew my weakness, an MTV Best Kiss, Rachel and Ryan style.

I gave in completely. I mean I seriously lost myself for a second. My hands clutched his shirt tightly, my brain went fuzzy, my skin regained its warmth. Were we at a high school dance? Ha! As if I even knew anymore. I might as well be on Jupiter.

His lips left mine and trailed down my neck. I caught my breath and realized his hands were clasped firmly on my chest. That was new. His mouth caught mine again and he let go of one of my breasts to grab my hand and place it in his lap.

Wait.

I forgot how to kiss. This was far past my experience level, and my whole body flushed at what I thought he might be trying to do.

"Come on," he murmured into my mouth, pressing my hand firmly into his groin. "Don't you want me?"

That wasn't a fair question, I thought. Too stunned to move or kiss back, he pulled away and started to unbelt and unzip his pants. I sunk back into my seat, feeling oddly like I was on a Tilt-A-Whirl, chest tight.

"I don't want to do this," I said stiffly, shaking a little.

He rolled his eyes. "Ingrid, it's not that hard. I'll show you."

He tried to guide my hands back onto him, but I pulled away out of sheer panic. "I don't want to do this, Corey."

He was becoming impatient, his normally handsome face dark and almost scary. My eyes welled up without me realizing and all of a sudden everything was blurry. He took the opportunity to swoop back in and kiss me, trying to pull me back under his waves again. But it was messy and unconvincing and then he grabbed the back of my head and yanked my face into his lap.

I released a high-pitched scream that startled him enough to release me, and flew back across the jeep, tumbling out the door.

"What the fuck, Ingrid!" Corey yelled out the open door. I pulled my shoes off the floor of his jeep and backed away on trembling legs.

"I said I didn't want to do that and you didn't listen," I stuttered out through choppy breaths. My throat burned from my scream and a tear slipped down my cheek and started to freeze in place but I hardly noticed the cold.

"Are you trying to get me fucking arrested screaming like that?" He seethed as he fumbled with his pants.

"That wasn't okay, Corey," I told him, this time more firmly. My heart pounded in my chest like I'd run a mile, and I couldn't stop heaving.

He laughed hysterically and pulled the keys out of his ignition. "Oh? I bet you fuck Hugo, though. Can't give me head, but I bet you go down on him like a pro. Slut."

My mouth dropped open in shock and disbelief.

"Oh my god, Corey," I wailed, throwing my arms into the air and practically sobbing. "It's psychotic!" I screeched. "I can't do this anymore! It's never been about Hugo! You make it about him! I feel like I'm going crazy. You can't be the one. You aren't who I thought!"

"You want to talk about false advertising, Ingrid?" He asked, a crazy frenzy taking over his entire demeanor. "If you're going to parade around like a slut, at least follow through!"

I slammed his door shut and in all my rage and disappointment, I lifted both of my middle fingers as I stormed away. "We're DONE. Stay away from me!"

In all my life I never looked at a boy and saw a monster. But I saw one tonight.

My feelings shifted, my world shattered. I walked into a new kind of reality and realized I was no longer in elementary school, or middle school. Frog Girl didn't exist, she was made up by children—and I wasn't surrounded by children anymore. Guys didn't like you, they lusted after you. They didn't want to love you, they just wanted a piece of you.

How had I lived so long in a delusion?

"You know what, Ingrid?" Corey hung out his window, banging on his jeep to get my attention. "They just wanted to see who could bang you first! I bet your precious Hugo didn't tell you that part. They said, "I bet that girl's easy!" and he didn't say a damn thing!"

"Leave me alone!" I screamed into the sky furiously.

There wasn't much dignity to salvage, but I didn't turn back. I put one foot in front off the other until I reached the door. My feet were icicles and my legs practically purple, but I staggered into the closest restroom. And only after I was locked safely away behind a stall door did I begin to sob uncontrollably, gasping and snotty and high-pitched.

I thought I'd been heartbroken before, but this time I really felt my heart crack into two. I once looked at that boy like he put stars in the sky. I let him pull me away from my friends. I told myself he was my prince. And it was all a joke. It was all a game. I had never been so mortified and humiliated.

My stomach pinched and churned, and I thought I might be sick. I felt itchy, like I needed to scrub every one of his touches off my skin. I fell onto the floor and buried my face in my knees, wishing desperately to just disappear.

The door crashed open and some giggling and chatter filled the room until they heard my weeping and hushed themselves.

"Hello? Hey? You okay in there?"

I watched two pairs of nylon clad feet shuffle in front of my stall door. Someone knocked.

"Do you need help?" The other girl asked, and it was her voice I recognized.

Sniffing, I stood and unlocked the stall door. I frantically started wiping away mascara tears just in time to come face to face with Cheyanna and a girl friend I didn't recognize.

Her mouth dropped open and she reached out to push a blonde curl out of my face. "Oh my god, Ingrid? Where's Corey?" She paused, and her frown lines deepened. "What the hell did he do to you?"

"It doesn't matter. We broke up," I told her hoarsely.

Her friend reached under her arm for her purse and began pulling out tissues and lip gloss. "Trust me, hon. You need these," she told me.

I grabbed the tissue from her and started cleaning up all the mascara and snot. Slowly, my breathing was evening out again.

Cheyanna rubbed my arm and started fixing my hair for me. "Was he your ride? Do you have a phone or someone here to take you home? If not, I'm sure Hannah will help you," she told me, nodding to her friend. Hannah gave me a warm smile.

"I have someone, it's okay," I said, sniffing. "But thank you. You guys are so nice."

Just their concern was enough to cause another breakdown.

"Are you sure?" She asked.

I nodded.

"Lipgloss," Hannah ordered. I took the tube from her and brushed some on. "Much better."

Cheyanna weaved her arm through mine. "Here I'll walk you out if you want."

I shook my head. "No that's okay. I have to find my friend."

"Okay."

She let me go and both her and Hannah watched me make my way to the exit.

"Hey, Ingrid."

I glanced back at her and she gave me an all-knowing look that made my heart flutter, like she saw right through me. Like she had been where I was.

"Not all guys are like that. Corey's an asshole."

I wasn't sure I was totally convinced, but she was right. Corey sucked. I smiled softly and left them.

The dance was in max party mode when I stepped back into the gymnasium. It looked like most of the school was there now, and they all jumped and danced chaotically among each other. You might have thought nothing else could possibly be going on at the same time. But you'd be wrong.

I started making my way towards the bleachers, but I realized almost immediately that Hugo was gone, and my heart deflated. I needed him. I missed him. Where was he? I dreaded the thought that he had left.

Disoriented, I looked toward the outskirts of the crowd. First, I saw Josie twirling in circles alongside Micah and his boyfriend. And right there next to them I was relieved to spot a tall, uncoordinated Hugo standing mostly in one place while Fiona tried to dance with him.

Any other day, I'd find Fiona repulsive, but I was too emotionally exhausted to feel anything but indifference. I just made a beeline for Hugo.

"Ingrid?"

Josie sounded breathless, but she was at my side in a second, practically hanging off me in concern.

"Have you been crying? Where have you been?"

Fiona noticed me next, and she pulled on Hugo's sleeve to get his attention. And when Hugo saw me, his expression dropped.

Pulling out of Fiona's grasp, he strode over and ducked down to get a better look at my eyes. His jaw clenched. All the years I'd known Hugo, he was anti-confrontation. But now his hands balled up into fists and he looked at me like a hitman with a mission.

"Where's Corey?" He asked.

Josie's eyes widened, and she cautiously backed away from me, glancing between us worriedly.

I shook my head. "The last time I saw him he was in his jeep. He's probably gone now."

He ignored the last part and made to storm off after him, but I stepped in front of him pleadingly, putting both hands up to stop him.

"It's over, Hugo. Don't make things worse. Please."

He looked down at me, the heat still in his eyes and a frown so deep and saddened I thought he might burst into tears himself.

"I hate him, Ingrid," he told me.

"I hate him too," I said. The cool composure I crafted before walking out of the restroom cracked as I stared up at him. I couldn't remember the last time things felt normal between us. My lips trembled, eyes welling up again. "And I miss you. And I'm sorry."

Without even hesitating he bent down and scooped me into a spine-crushing hug. It didn't matter that I could hardly breathe or that people were staring or that I was crying uncontrollably all over again. I was just so happy to have Hugo.

All I wanted was him.

Chapter 21

There are two crucial periods in a person's dating life. Up until this point I was in my happy, fairy tale world I now refer to as B.C. (Before Corey). But after the dumpster fire that was our break-up, I now lived in the depressing new age A.C. (After Corey). And in this world, love felt impossible. I never thought I'd get those joyful fluttering feelings of romantic wonder ever again.

Not even The Notebook helped. Normally, I cried watching the love between Allie and Noah bloom and come to fruition. It made me crave all things heart-shaped and glittery. But A.C. I watched the entire movie with a blank, unfeeling stare.

My mom even went into break-up mode with me. Movie marathon, pizza, ice cream, helping me destroy all things Corey—and nothing. She looked at me like I transformed into a different person overnight. But her concern had nothing on Hugo.

"Please," Hugo begged the day after homecoming at his parent's bakery. He helped me load fresh loafs of bread into the display case and was continuously denting every loaf he picked up. "Can't you be careful with your heart for once? If not for yourself then for me?"

He had been going off on one of his tangents for a while, but now I peered up at him curiously. "Why for you?"

He paused and took a breath, shifting his weight back to look down at me properly. "Because it hurts me to see you hurt, and I'm tired of hurting like this all the time."

"Hugo..."

"Take it from someone who actually loves you," he interrupted gently. "Maybe it's time to take a break from this."

I was planning on taking a break anyway, so I just nodded. It wasn't like me to do things the Hugo way, but the whole Corey experience changed everything. Even though it went against everything I believed in, I had to slow down. If Corey taught me anything, it was that some opportunities are okay to miss. In fact, just don't take them at all. Ever. Save yourself.

I was focused on me, now. Me and my friends. I was done kissing frogs.

"So, Pete's pretty nice. Makes good popcorn," Hugo said to break up the silence we'd been sitting in for the past hour while watching Parks & Recreation.

"Yeah, he's alright." I shrugged. "He'll probably make you coffee in the morning too. That's, like, his ritual. My mom hasn't touched the coffee maker since he moved in."

"Huh."

Again, silence. Hugo was doing that thing where he psyches himself up for a conversation. I was trying to ignore it. The night was going so well, and I could already tell he was thinking of some way to bring it up.

And then...

"Are you ever going to tell me what happened that night?" Hugo asked while oh-so-casually propping his chin up in his hand. "It's been months. I won't lose my cool."

Knew it.

I changed the channel boredly and shoved a handful of popcorn in my mouth. "Oh, something tells me you'll lose your cool."

He launched an M&M at me. "You know, that only makes me assume the worst."

Groaning, I pulled myself out of our blanket fort and crossed my living room to rummage through the DVD collection. "Can't you just trust me when I say it doesn't matter?"

He poked his head out of the blanket fort just to make sure I could see his expression which was both unimpressed and dripping with skepticism.

"No actually, because you haven't been yourself since," he reasoned. "At first I thought it was your normal break up blues, but now it's just eerie. We didn't even watch Mama Mia! and every time I sleep over here you make me watch it. I know the songs, Ingrid. Every word."

"Well you're in luck because I've got the DVD right here," I told him, latching onto any opportunity to change the subject. I turned on my toes and waved the movie around with an impish grin. I had to show him I was fine.

Hugo knew better than to pry about things I didn't want to talk about. He was much better at that than I ever was. But, lately he made a habit of asking about the break up every couple of weeks and I was beginning to understand how annoying it could be.

I didn't tell anyone about jeep incident. Not my mom not Josie and especially not Hugo. It was embarrassing. Getting your face held down in someone's lap? Not a story you want to share. Having your boyfriend scream out his car window that the entire soccer team was all wagering on who'd get the opportunity to have sex with you first? Also gross and unfun to talk about.

I didn't want talk about it ever.

"And if you're really that worried, we can have some girl talk right now," I teased, allowing some of my old craziness to seep back in. "Tell me about your mystery lady. You know, the one you're waiting to smooch."

His cheeks rosied up real quick at that, but he recovered quickly with the clearing of his throat and then disappeared back underneath the blanket. "Fine, don't tell me," he said. "It's fine. Clearly, it's none of my business. And since we're on the subject of none of your business, I'm not talking about that either."

I giggled. "Why not, Hugo? I think it's so romantic."

"Shut up!'

I tiptoed back to the fort and flung myself inside, tackling him with a muffled squeal. He yelled in surprise and looped an arm around my waist to try and pull me off. "Jesus, Ingrid!"

I tossed the DVD to the side and pinned down his shoulders so that he couldn't hide his face when I started questioning him.

"Is it Fiona?" I pestered with a breathless giggle.

He stopped his struggling and looked up at me with a goofy grin, fingers drumming against my hip. "You're so obsessed with her."

I rolled my eyes. My heart didn't pound at the thought of them anymore. He told me to ditch him, so I ditched him while I was dating Corey. If some other girl came into his life that he got along with while I was gone, I wasn't allowed to be upset. I was weird around Josie at first too. I had to learn how to cope with Hugo branching out.

"Oh, come on. She totally likes you. Besides, just because I'm in a slump, doesn't mean you should be." When no gut-wrenching feeling swept through me, I knew I meant it.

He watched me carefully as I said that, and it reminded me of all the times Corey looked at me when he talked about Hugo. That made a shiver go through me.

I quickly rolled off him and picked up the DVD, feeling very uncomfortable with that.

Stupid.

Hugo sat up and took the DVD from me so I couldn't distract myself while he talked to me. If he was confused, he didn't show it. I don't know how he did that.

"I'm telling you, as my best friend whom I would never lie to," he told me earnestly. "It's not her."

I nodded. Maybe he thought that's what I wanted to hear. It was impossible to tell him what was really going on in my head, so there was no point telling him Corey made that face when he was searching for a lie. Like he wanted there to be a lie too.

Hugo isn't Corey. Hugo isn't Corey.

"So are we going to watch this or...?" He held up Mama Mia!.

I took a breath and worked the smile back onto my face.

"We have to," I said, chipper again as I snatched back the DVD. "You know all the words. We're going to sing Dancing Queen."

He tried to look upset, but after the third time watching this movie with him, I knew he secretly loved it. Besides, I needed to do a better job of acting normal. If singing ABBA was how it had to be done, then so be it.

Hugo fell asleep halfway through the movie, so I turned it off and tried to get comfortable on the floor beside him. We should have used the couch cushions as a makeshift mattress instead of walls, but it had been ages since we'd built one, so we'd lost our touch.

He snored softly, and his lankly limbs were at in all sorts of uncomfortable looking angles so he'd fit inside. I watched him breathe for a minute, hoping the rise and fall of his chest would lull me to sleep. But, my eyes kept shifting back to his face.

I had my mom and I had him. Those were the two people I loved and trusted most in the world, and the fact that I hadn't told them anything about Corey was eating me up. It was making me paranoid. I felt horrible.

I wanted to be free of it.

Of course, three o'clock in the morning is when one starts feeling really weird and existential. And it was exactly five after.

I scooted closer and scanned his face to make sure he was truly asleep. And then I finally told my secret.

"I think he sort of assaulted me," I whispered into the dark. Hugo continued to snore. "And I'm afraid if I say it out loud it will make it real."

It was a release, a weight off my chest. And smiled to myself in that moment, knowing even though he couldn't hear me, that I told someone.

"Goodnight, Hugo."

And then I drifted off to the sound of his breathing, feeling more at peace now than I had in months.

Chapter 22

When Hugo and I started learning how to drive, it was the most dangerous thing to happen in our town since the tornado that ripped through twenty years earlier. I basically required a police escort I was so tragic, and Hugo had what they call "bricks for feet". I never pegged him for a NASCAR driver, but once that kid hit the gas he forgot what brakes were.

"I was going to buy you a car but now I'm afraid of what you'll do to the mailbox," Mom joked one day after a pretty awful driving lesson. "Hugo's mom was so close to never having to drive you two to school ever again. So close."

"I've still got plenty of time before my sixteenth birthday. I'm gonna become a pro, you'll see," I told her with faux-confidence, but I was pretty sure I was screwed.

"Maybe Peter can take you driving one of these days. He's a better driver than me and could probably wrangle you easier too," she suggested.

And that's how I ended up with Peter in the passenger's seat of my mom's Prius.

He was pretty chill. I didn't hang around him all that often—too much teen angst to juggle—but he didn't seem like the kind to lose his cool if I accidentally drove us into a stop sign.

Besides his receding hairline he was alright looking. Pretty bland. He kind of reminded me of Patrick Day in that way. Kind of soft and squishy. Harmless. The sideburns he was rocking didn't suit him, but I was in no place to be telling a forty-something-year-old man that his facial hair was gnarly, so I settled for just staring at them in stupefaction every time I remembered they were there.

"Alright, Grid." Ah, the warm-up speech. I let my fingers dance over the steering wheel to release some nervous jitters. "Driving is easy. Like riding a bike. You know how to ride a bike?"

"Sure do."

"Easy-peasy, right?" He said. "Little wobbly at first, but now you're a pro."

He wasn't wrong.

I listened to his advice which wasn't different yet somehow less condescending than when my mother explained it. Slowly apply pressure to the gas and brake pedals. Slowly turn the wheel.

Same lessons, different execution, and a star was born.

I slowly pulled out of the driveway and took Peter's nonsensical directions all around town. My mother panicked every time I touched the gas pedal, Peter lounged in the passenger seat and had a conversation with me.

Peter was cool.

"So your mom kind of confused me when she explained your relationship with that boy Hugo," he said all of a sudden at a stoplight.

Once upon a time I would have lifted my foot right off the brake and rolled into the car in front of us at the mere mention of my friendship with Hugo being anything else. These days I was less excitable, and honestly, not even all that annoyed.

"He's been my friend since the first grade," I told him simply. "We're like family with the Guerra's."

"Yeah, so how did that happen?" He asked curiously, scratching at those god awful sideburns. "Your mom was telling me things were rough after the divorce and his family absorbed yours without a second thought."

The light switched green and I held my breath as I slowly pressed down on the gas pedal. "Well," I said through a smile at my success. "As Hugo says, they're Italian. Everyone's family."

Peter chuckled to himself. "Hugo's quiet for a little Italian boy."

I snorted at that. "Trust me, the rest of the Guerra's are not."

"You know, that's something to consider when you're dating someone. The family. If the family sucks it's probably not going to work out," he told me.

My eyebrows twitched together. What was he talking about?

"I'm just saying, if Hugo's family is your family, I would love to come to one of your joint family dinners," he proposed. "I have a feeling they're going to be a part of your lives for a long time and since I want to marry your mother, I'd love to be included in that."

I glanced over at him with a smile I couldn't stop from blooming across my face. Where did my mom find this guy? Peter wasn't just cool, he was the kind of guy I hoped she would always marry.

"Really?" I asked. "You want to meet the Guerra's?"

He smiled back at me and then signaled for me to put my attention back on the road. "I want to be a part of your family, so yes I do."

I laughed to myself a little, and released a sigh of relief as I settled back against the seat. "Wow, I'm so glad you just wanted to come to dinner. For a second I thought you were going to ask if Hugo was my boyfriend."

Peter waved his hand dismissively. "No. I talked to Hugo one morning after he slept over because he kind of hung around a lot and I thought to myself, wow, that's really trusting of your mom to let your boyfriend sleep over at the house. And then Hugo assured me you two were just friends. But, you know, he did sound a little disappointed when he said it. It was early, though. Maybe he was just tired."

"Probably just tired," I agreed instantly. "He's got this mystery girl he won't tell me about. Doesn't make sense, though. Because I can count on my hand the girls he knows, and the math doesn't add up." I wanted to roll my eyes just thinking about that conundrum.

"Turn here," Peter instructed. I did as I was told and as soon as the turn was completed he was diving back into the conversation like a teenager. "Why doesn't the math add up?"

I snorted. "Because Hugo talks to three girls. One, Fiona, he assured me was definitely not the one. I'm ninety-nine percent sure he's telling the truth even though they get along well. Next girl is Josie, but she's a little much for him and they have completely opposite interests. He kind of has to take Josie in doses, which leads me to believe that she's not it either."

I could see Peter smiling largely out of the corner of my eye which made me glance at him suspiciously. "What?"

"That, presumably, leaves you as the final girl," Peter announced. He behaved as though he thought I hadn't considered that. But I had.

"Yes, that leaves me. But that doesn't make sense either," I told him with unshakeable confidence.

"Careful for the pothole!"

Thunk!

"Next time try to miss those."

I grimaced but made a mental note.

He looked to me with an anticipation I hardly expected to see from my mother's boyfriend. Why was I discussing this with him?

"So why doesn't it make sense?" He prompted, quickly forgetting about the pothole.

"Because it's been, like, ten years," I told him with an increasing amount of excitement building in my voice. It was so obvious. "If he liked me, why didn't he just say something?"

"Maybe he didn't know he could," Peter suggested. "You know, I was friends with your mom before we started dating. She was going on all these blind dates and I thought, wow, she must hate the guys she already knows if she's willing to be subjected to that."

I looked at him incredulously. "But you didn't ask her out, though. She probably thought nobody she knew was interested in her."

"Ah-ha! See," Peter said, lifting a finger as though ready to make some dramatic point. "We were assuming things. Alright, now pull into the driveway nice and easy."

I stared at the garage door for a couple of seconds after putting the car in park. I wouldn't say I was considering what Peter said to be a truth bomb, but I was certainly trying to put pieces together in my head to see if they made sense.

"I'll let your mom know I'm coming to the joint dinner this week," Peter said, popping the passenger side door open. "I think you should think about Hugo."

Well now it was impossible not to.

It had been so long since I touched my Possible Princes Journal that Corey wasn't even an entry all done up in hearts. I sat on the floor of my bedroom and bounced it between my hands. I remembered picking it out from the drugstore near the movie theatre that had since been torn down. Of course, alterations were made. Puffy paints and glitter crumbled off the cover and onto my fingers, and I smiled to myself at the memory.

I opened the cover and laughed at the slanted, five-year-old handwriting scrawled across the page in bright red ink.

INGRID'S DAIRY. DO NOT OPEN.

I ran my fingers over the misspelling and turned the pages. Benjamin, Clayton, Zak/Violet, Micah, Patrick...

I'd printed out school pictures or online profiles. I'd saved Reese's wrappers and love letters. Wedding details from my dress to the flowers changed from boy to boy. A big red X crossed over each and every failure, except for Clayton who'd been tossed in the trash so long ago. Just a torn-out gap remained where he was meant to be.

One of the last entries I'd ever written was a list I seemed to have forgotten.

Terms and Conditions of the Prince

1. Stays

2 Is, in fact, an actual boy and not a faker on Myspace

3. Isn't ashamed to be seen with me

4. Nice

5. Doesn't take me for granted

6. Believes in true love

7. Looks at me like Hugo's parents look at each other

8. Listens

9. Someone who won't make me cry (unless it's happy tears because that's a good thing)

10. Hugs better than a blanket burrito

I sighed heavily and closed the book. I should have followed my terms and conditions.

Peter said to think about Hugo. And honestly, I was aware that boy ticked all my boxes. But Hugo was my friend first before anything else. The couple times he'd made my heart flutter, he seemed to realize it and quickly smashed the moment with a hammer. He had a way of ruining that kind of thing.

Even though he went along with my pact he did it under the pretense that I'd end up with someone else anyway. It's easy to agree to something when you believe there's a guarantee it won't happen.

So what was the point of concerning myself with this at all? I still wasn't myself. I hadn't looked at a boy like that in half a year. I just wanted that those feeling back. That's all.

And if it happened to be Hugo that made me feel all those things again?

Well, that was fate. And I couldn't argue with that.

When Peter met the Guerra's it became less of a casual Wednesday dinner and more of a world-class celebration. Hugo's family put their best spread out—a feast I'd only seen on Christmas or Easter. It was mind boggling the amount of side dishes and desserts that were available.

Peter was bombarded with all sorts of questions. Where did he grow up? What was his family like? How did he meet my mom? How did he ask her out?

Adults are basically oversized teenagers, and they gossip like them too.

Hugo and I sat side-by-side on the bench seat as usual. The adults all laughed and talked over one another, sipping a deep red wine every time they stopped to take a breath.

Nonna's laugh rang at the highest pitch. She may not have been able to speak clear English, but she loved to show everyone that she understood everything they were saying.

I happily scooped a bite into my mouth and turned to Hugo. He was watching the conversation, but mostly keeping comments to himself. When he noticed my gaze, he smiled a little.

"Always so loud," he said quietly with a short laugh.

I grinned at him fondly, an old memory of a similar dinner the night my mom and I came over the first time crossed my mind.

"It's perfect," I told him, patting his arm. "I love our family."

His cheeks went pink and his eyes swept around the table. I followed his eyes. Peter fell against the back of Maria's old chair and clutched my mother's shoulder as he laughed at something Hugo's dad said. My mother nearly spit out her drink and Mrs. Guerra now stood and hurried to the kitchen to dole out desserts. I looked back at him and he seemed to frown to himself.

"Do you think it's going to be like this ten years from now?" He asked, almost regretful.

I tilted my head inquisitively. "Do you want it to be?"

He looked around the table again and nodded.

"Then it's going to be exactly like this ten years from now," I promised.

A pleased smile spread across his cheeks and he wrapped an arm around my shoulder, pulling me close with a content-ed sigh. It was a good place to be.

I guess when you know someone for so long you get used to the way they smell or they way they make you feel and you just take it for granted. You never even think about what would happen if you didn't have it. But in that moment, I remembered Hugo smelled like cinnamon body wash he probably stole from Maria, and under the weight of his arm I felt warm and safe.

I almost flinched at the realization, because it felt like he just stomped his heavy brick foot onto the gas pedal of my heart.

Chapter 23

I thought the sudden shift in feelings for Hugo would pass the way it did a couple years ago, but it only got embarrassingly worse. It was weird feeling again after Corey, and the jumpstart to my heart electrified every moment with Hugo the second it happened. It was almost overwhelming, and honestly, terrifying.

Things between us sometimes didn't just feel comfortable, they felt overtly sensual. I stopped doing things like jumping on him for hugs and kissing his cheek. Now it just felt wrong. His long meaningful looks made goosebumps appear all over. His self-deprecating humor that once made me roll my eyes now made my heart soften like butter in the microwave on HIGH.

All I wanted to do was stroke his arm and run my fingers though his hair and, you know, cuddle for eternity. I fantasized the way he would declare his love for me in scenarios beyond the realm of certain possibility. He was a farmhand and I a beautiful but untouchable European duchess. He was the softhearted pirate who taught my siren soul to love. We survived the Hunger Games together.

I'd daydreamed it all.

But for the first time in all my life, I was absolutely, positively, not going to tell him. I wasn't even hinting that I was all heart-eyes. I couldn't just freak him out like that. This was a delicate situation, okay? Even if Peter was right and Hugo was secretly harboring a crush on me, I couldn't just throw it on him now. After Corey? He'd think I was officially broken and grasping at straws.

And you know what? I was okay with it. I'd just pine after him like a normal person. That's tragic and romantic, right?

If we truly were bound by fate, then I'd done my part and finally fallen. She was more than welcome to do the rest.

I was too nervous anyway. We all have our limits.

Besides, it was the summer before our sophomore year. We were elbow deep in Italian baked goods and driving lessons. There were other things to worry about.

"I don't think I can do soccer this year," Hugo told me one late afternoon while he wiped down the countertops at The Bread Basket in preparation for closing. "He's a senior this year and probably a team captain so I'll pass, for sure."

I was refilling a napkin dispenser and smiled to myself at his refusal to call Corey out by name.

"So," I prompted. "Are you actually going to join a club or..."

"I was thinking maybe the swim team would be alright. I'm not the worst swimmer. Maybe I'll grow a bicep." He shrugged and threw the towel over his shoulder.

I paused, considering this. Now, I don't know if you've ever seen a swimmer before. We're talking shoulder muscles. We're talking abs for days. Eat, sleep, swim kinda people.

They live solely on spaghetti diets and Gatorade. They talk like gang members. One word: speedos.

There was no way, no way, Hugo was joining the swim team.

Taking a stack of napkins in my hand, I carefully pushed them into place and said, "Are you sure? The swim team is kind of...intense."

Again, he shrugged. "Like I said, maybe I'll grow a bicep."

Something like that was way too silly to make me blush, or so I thought. Hugo? Dripping wet? In a speedo? Biceps? I should've laughed, but all I could do was sit in God-fearing silence. This was the end. The end of my sanity.

"Really, I'm doing you a favor," he said casually, almost teasingly. "You can come to my meets and check out all the shirtless guys you want. This is my gift to you."

I wanted to choke. "Great."

He came to lean on the counter where I was sitting and looked at me oddly. "You good?"

I nodded, not looking at him. Lately he felt so close. Like, jeez, if I turn my head I might "accidentally" kiss you.

"Yeah, you know, you don't have to do that. I'm over Corey. I'm over all of it. I'm good, great. You should just join the sewing club and call it a day."

He snorted and pinched my arm lightly. I let my eyes slide his direction, immediately regretting it. Just some normal, unsexy eye contact made my stomach flip. And, really, he was way too close. I could just lean in and...

His warm brown eyes swept over my face and I held my breath. "I'm just making a joke, Ingrid. About the guys. I just want to get in shape. For me."

Maybe he thought I was still fragile from the breakup or whatever. I was for a long time, but now I was just anxious about him. Everything he did was fireworks.

I released the air caught in my throat and turned my attention back to the napkins.

"Okay," I said, because what else should I say?

If Hugo sensed anything different, he didn't let it show. Though suggesting he join a near-naked sport right to my face did make me wonder. But he wasn't like that, so I slid off the counter and put the full napkin dispenser where it belonged beside the cash register.

Hugo watched me skirt around him and busy myself with adjusting the shoulder straps on my apron. For a minute or two I felt his gaze, heavy as his brick feet, observe my careful avoidance.

"You want to...talk about something?" His voice lilted curiously, begging me to unravel all of my secrets.

Okay, so he obviously sensed a change.

I fiddled with the apron strap for another second and sighed hopelessly as I fell against the back counter.

"How do you read me so well? It's annoying sometimes."

The corners of his mouth turned up slightly in a small grin. "Almost ten years of friendship will do that." He let that sink in for a moment, and then, "So, what's up?"

The thing about being head-over-heels for your best friend is that you have to be really, really sure it's not just...loneliness.

I slid onto the counter and let my dangling legs swing. "Do we feel different to you?"

He pulled the towel off his shoulder and folded it sloppily before setting it next to him with what felt like his hundredth shrug of the day.

"What do you mean?" He asked, this time being the one of us that maintains steady, unwavering eye contact instead of staring at his feet.

"You know, different. Like kind of tense...lately." I was hoping he'd take a hint, but either he was playing dumb or not in the same shifting universe I was in because he just looked at me blankly in reply. "No?"

He scratched the back of his head and glanced to the giant store windows. The sun had turned orange but still hung high in the sky, casting strange shadows along the tile floor.

"I just thought it was a delayed side-effect of him," he said softly. "Is it something else? Did I do something?"

I shook my head frantically. "No, Hugo. God, no. It has nothing to do with Corey. Nothing's wrong, you didn't do anything."

Nodding, he crossed his arms and stared down at the floor, his eyes searching for words between the cracks until finally like a deflating balloon he said, "Well then, yeah. You've been acting weird. There, I said it."

Me? Just me? There wasn't more to it? He didn't feel the need to shy away himself?

Well, that was short-lived. Time to abort.

I took a deep breath and gripped the counter. "Sorry. I'll fix it."

"So, you're not going to tell me why you're being weird?" Hugo asked, his eyebrows pinched together.

"You're weird sometimes too and I don't make you explain it," I retorted while untying my apron and sliding off the counter.

"Oh, do explain," he challenged in a way meant to sound playful, but his arms only tightened in the knot across his chest.

I stuffed the apron in the box under the counter and stood with a hand on my hip. "I don't want to rock the boat, Hugo. I've just had some revelations, as they say."

"About what?"

"You"

"Then I think I have a right to know," he told me all the more stubbornly.

Was it wrong that I found this bit of back and forth exciting? It was like being in his room again all those months ago, both standing mid-argument with an odd energy pulsing all around. It made me want to jump him.

"You know, really, it's Peter's fault. He put these ideas in my head. I can't be held responsible."

"Ingrid..."

"I think you were jealous sometimes. About the other guys."

He looked as though he was going to deny it, and then he anchored a hand on the counter beside him and licked his lips. "I was."

Well, what the hell.

"Wait, what?"

"You're my best friend, of course I didn't want you ditching me to be with someone else. I still have PTSD from Clayton, so..."

"That is so not what I meant." He quickly looked to his feet and swallowed a lump in his throat. "And you know it."

He looked back to me carefully, but his eyes swept over my face like he was trying to figure something out. We stood a step apart and he reached out to push my hair over my shoulder, his fingers lingering at my neck just barely brushing the skin. Goosebumps broke out across my arms.

"What exactly do you think you know?" He asked, his voice hushed. His hand remained in place for a moment and he looked me square in the eye.

What is going on?

I thought perhaps that moment was finally blooming right before my eyes. He seemed uncomfortable but steadily sure. His hand might be preparing to pull me to him. I licked my lips and tried to create that cinematic non-verbal conversation that would lead to that one romantic moment...but the kitchen door burst open like a wrecking ball.

Hugo jumped back and turned away, but I stood frozen as his father barreled into the room with his grandmother a couple steps in tow.

"Closing time," he sang blissfully, wrapping one arm around me and pulling a reluctant Hugo into his side with the other. "My two fabulous helpers, gather your things so we can go home."

I tried to catch Hugo's gaze again, to see if I'd imagined that whole scenario, but he kept his eyes to the floor even after his father released us and his grandmother had left to go start the car.

While I reached for my purse, he sorted through the money and locked the register. I had to remind him to take off his apron on our way out the door. The moment was over, dead-and I didn't even know if it was real.

We sat side-by-side in the red mini-van. He looked out the window and I stared out mine. I didn't know what he was thinking about, but I knew I was replaying what happened over and over in my head. I tried to imagine what it would have been like if I just stood on my toes and planted one on him. But the idea that he may have been thinking the very same thing, that he should've kissed me made my brain buzz deliriously.

I was all shook up like a pop can, ready to explode.

We didn't talk about it. Hugo pretended like it never even happened, which baffled me because in the moment he see med...confident? I wanted to talk about it, though. I wanted to finish the conversation. Was I right in thinking I was his mystery girl? That one little moment pretty much confirmed that suspicion-but I wanted to hear him say it. I wanted him to tell me how he felt.

Weeks passed, our sophomore year started, and Hugo was on full lockdown after that day in the bakery. Understandably, I was wound tight and stuck somewhere between not wanting to say something and make things weirder, and randomly showing up at the Guerra residence at midnight with a love ballad and a boombox to kickstart this whole thing.

I was starting to think I imagined everything. I created some uncomfortable moment that we would never be able to face. Before, I was the one that pulled back. Now he could hardly look me in the eye without blushing. Our sleepovers were few and far between.

"I miss him," I whined to Josie one day at passing time. She didn't know the details on mine and Hugo's weird friendship right now, but she noticed we weren't our usual selves.

"What happened anyway? Did you guys finally make out and it was super awkward or...?" She asked hungrily, pouncing on the opportunity to learn the juicy gossip Hugo and I weren't talking about. Her auburn curls bounced as she walked, and she leaned in close to make sure she didn't miss a single detail.

"Nothing really happened," I told her, but she squealed at even that much information. "In fact, it's the not happening that's making us sort of distant and...ugh!"

She stared at me hard, trying to piece together this very vague information, but she was a bloodhound, and pretty much had it all figured out before I finished my sentence.

"You two are such dummies. You're totally pining for each other-and not just now, but since, like, forever. God, just have babies already."

I shoved her and she giggled. "I so knew it. He was being so weird and you're clearly walking on eggshells trying not to do or say the wrong thing. I'll talk to him. As soon as he knows for sure you've got a big fat crush on him, he'll stop being such a coward."

I frowned. "He's not a coward. And please do not do that. It'll freak him out. I think I already freaked him out. I knew this would happen. I should have kept my mouth shut."

"Oh, so you already told him?"

I made a face. "Not exactly. We really didn't say much now that I think about it. It was a lot of eye contact. And me wishing he'd just kiss me already."

My whole face burned red at that confession, one I'd never said out loud before. Josie skipped as she walked, squealing and giggling and being so embarrassing I wanted to sink into the floor.

"Oh my god, please let me say something. Or at least hint. Please!" She begged pathetically as she hung from my shoulder. "I've been invested in this too long."

I shook my head. "I sort of think it should come from me."

"Well then hurry up, because you told the wrong person if you're thinking of keeping this a secret. In fact, maybe that's why you finally said something. You need a consequence." She bit her lip mischievously. "If you don't say something soon, I will. Tick, tock." And with that, she disappeared into her next class, leaving me with a racing heart and a pink face.

Well, I had no choice now. It was confession time.

Chapter 24

Setting the scene for a love confession isn't nearly as romantic as you might think. Mostly, it's worrying that you're either going to be coming on way too strong or that you'll be so subtle your love won't realize you just revealed the most vulnerable contents of your heart. I had to tailor this moment to fit Hugo, the most love-starved person in all the world. A former non-believer, an amateur in romance, a timid baby bird in this whole new world. One wrong move and I feared Hugo would avoid me for the rest of our days.

I could organize a sleepover—that seemed the riskiest. Confessing secrets to each other in the dead of the night? Sure, seems like the obvious choice, but alas if something goes catastrophically wrong, we'd be forced to be together until well into the morning sitting in an uncomfortable stew of tension and hormones. No thanks.

Perhaps I'd just blurt it out, a good old fashion yell it from the rooftops. Quick, painless, like ripping off a fresh bandage. But more than likely I'd be met with hard denial and refusal. He would think I've completely lost my mind. It just looks crazy, you know?

So, I asked him to see a movie with me. Not a matinee, because that screams "we're just friends" in the most obvious way ever, but to an evening showing—classy. The movie would let out just early enough that we could decide whether it was too awkward to hang out afterward or not.

Of course, I didn't explicitly tell him this was a date because...was it? No, it was an opportunity to make a move.

At least that's what I told the butterflies in my stomach as I waited at the door for the Guerra minivan. Hugo had just got his license (to everyone's surprise and relief), and he insisted on driving us to our first ever outing without parental escort. This wasn't a planned convenience, but I took it as a sign from God that this was meant to be.

Was I slightly terrified that he might wreck and kill us before I got the chance to tell him what was up? Yes, I was absolutely horrified at the very real possibility that that very thing could happen.

Happy thoughts, positive thoughts.

"Well, don't you look nice."

I glanced anxiously over my shoulder, and upon seeing Peter standing just outside the kitchen with a bowl of ice cream and a grin, I feigned a very Zen demeanor and looped my fingers in my belt loops.

"Thanks," I said, turning on my toes and rocking back. "Hugo's picking me up—by himself, no big deal."

Peter's grin went lopsided and he scooped himself a large spoonful of chocolate ice cream and balanced it in front of his face. "That's nice. Private."

I blinked several times in stupefaction of his heavy-handedness. He watched my face flush for a second. "Mmhmm." He hummed to himself, and took a bite as he walked toward the living room where my mother was watching something with an obnoxious laugh track.

The blaring of a car horn startled me out of my stunned state and I grabbed my purse and hurried out the door, heart thumping.

"It's Hugo, I'll be home later," I called over my shoulder.

"Home by ten!" My mom yelled back. But it was Peter's comment that echoed in my ears as I walked down the sidewalk toward the Guerra's red van.

"Don't have too much fun!"

Hugo and I sat side-by-side in a slowly filling theater. He picked at the popcorn and I tried not to sit like a stone statue beside him. The car ride was quiet, mostly just chat about what movie we were seeing. He insisted on paying for both tickets at the window, which only made me more jelly-legged than I already was.

There was no reason to be nervous, this was Hugo. We'd done this a hundred times before. But, I'd picked a sweater with a lower neckline than normal, so then I panicked and let my hair do it's own slightly wavy, slightly curly bird's nest thing that it does when I don't touch it because I didn't want to look like I was trying too hard.

Hugo's leg bounced, and I looked over to him. He had a fresh hair-cut, but that's really the only thing noteworthy. He looked cool, calm, collected. Except for that bouncing leg.

"You wanna do anything after this?" I asked.

He leaned his forearm on the arm rest between us and turned his face toward me, suddenly close. I tried to look unbothered, but I know I glanced at his lips.

"I don't know, maybe," he said. "When do you have to be back, ten?"

I nodded, noticing the mouthwash on his breath. My chest seized up and I looked back toward the screen.

It was weird, the whole trying to be casual thing. It didn't really feel like we were succeeding, but wasn't that intentional? I couldn't even think anymore.

When the lights dimmed and the theater went silent, I tried to focus on making sure my breathing pattern was normal. Previews came and went, the beginning of the film got lost in overthinking. I kept looking at him from the corner of my eye.

His arm was still on that arm rest between us, and his hand dangled onto my side. Was it on purpose?

I've never had to psych myself up for something like this before, I was a born natural. I chased frogs. I chased boys. I...

Held my breath and curled my index finger around his. His leg, which had been bouncing throughout the duration of the movie, suddenly stopped. And I swore our eyes met when we glanced sideways at each other. Both frozen, I somehow mustered the courage to slide all of my fingers between his and hold his hand. We'd held hands before, if only to drag each other around or keep close in crowded areas, but never like this.

He quietly cleared his throat and released a long, shaky breath, but he didn't pull away. Instead, he sunk back in his seat and stiffly held my hand for the remainder of the movie. And when it was over, I gently let go of his hand and turned to see his face.

His eyes were soft and his expression almost sad as we stared at each other in the dimmed theater, trying to decide where we'd go from there.

"I think I want to go to our old playground," I told him. "We could sit on your bench."

The corner of his mouth twitched up in what looked to be the beginning of a smile. "Okay."

We pulled up to our old school for the first time in years. It was mostly dark except for some streetlights illuminating the merry-go-round and monkey bars. I was suddenly reminded of the time spent chasing boys across the rocks or watching games of Red Rover from the sidelines.

I followed Hugo to his old bench, now more rickety than it was ten years ago and graffitied a bit. I wondered how many other kids sat here all recess waiting for the bell to ring the way Hugo did.

When we sat down, we looked out at the playground, remembering the screams and giggles of our classmates. Everything was so different now. Girls now twerked on social media and all those boys I tried to smooch were finding creative ways to throw parties in their parent's homes without getting caught. Sometimes it felt like the only people who hadn't changed were me and Hugo.

Beside me, Hugo sighed and leaned forward to rest his elbows on his knees. He shook his head and stared out at the swings. "What are you doing, Ingrid?" He asked after a few moments.

The skin on the back of my neck prickled and I felt my face warm. Now that we were here my stomach turned and I might as well have transformed into the Cowardly Lion. "I don't know what you mean..."

He scoffed and looked back at me, eyes not quite meeting mine. "I know it was weird what I did in the bakery that day, but you don't have to...do this."

I stared at him a minute, feeling my limbs go numb with nervousness. Alright, we were doing this. We were going for it, the talk. Us. We decided to be friends on this bench, but I couldn't remember the last time I saw him as just a friend. If I was being honest with myself, I was possessive of him even when I was with Corey, and that was an unexpected truth I never thought I'd admit.

"You haven't been paying attention if you think this starts with that day at the bakery," I finally told him.

He shook his head again and looked back out at the playground. There was an internal struggle going on there. His fingers were restless, and he couldn't look at me no matter how many times his head twitched like he might glance back. It was making me anxious.

All the tension and nervousness bubbled under my skin until finally I had to blurt out what I came here to say.

"I have a big, fat crush on you, Hugo," I said into the silence between us. I clenched my eyes shut, and every part of my body that could seize up and barricade itself in safety did just that. My toes curled, my fists balled up, and my shoulders nearly hugged my head. "I needed to tell you that before Josie did it for me."

I felt him lean back and I popped an eye open to gauge his reaction. His eyes rested on my lap and a once clenched jaw now softened as he smiled.

"She never would have actually said anything, you know," he told me. "She talks a big game, but she wouldn't do anything without permission."

I huffed and crossed my arms. "You don't know that."

He shrugged. "Well, she's been keeping my secret since middle school, but you're right, I wouldn't know."

I gasped, jolting forward at that. "Middle school? You kept this from me that long?" My mind spun. "How come you never said anything? You knew I was looking for someone who loved me, and you never said that."

He tucked a leg underneath him to gain some height and frowned as he turned toward me, his face serious. "Because it shouldn't be like that, Ingrid," he nearly scolded. "You should be with me because you want to, not just because I tell you something like that so you give me a chance. Everyone always said we should be together, and I hated it. I didn't want that to sway you towards me if you really didn't want me in the first place."

I groaned, throwing my hands up in exasperation. "It's not like that, I promise."

He put a hand up to stop me. "It's just...I never wanted to be the last resort. I used to think it wasn't that big of deal if we were really going to go through with that stupid pact, but you know what, it is a big deal. It is, because I deserve to be someone's first choice. I've loved one girl my whole life, but I don't want to be with her if she doesn't really want to be with me. You shouldn't feel obligated to be with me."

I melted at that, feeling all that sudden anger leave my body in a slow fizzle. I could only register one thing.

"You love me?"

He looked at me like I truly didn't know him at all. "Of course I love you. I've always loved you. Romantic or not. You know that."

It was a movie moment. We gazed at each other anew in the streetlight, a soft breeze tangled in our hair, and my heart beat to an indie song I hadn't even heard of yet.

"Look, I know it's hard to believe me when my whole life I've been chasing one boy after the next, but I'm done with that," I assured him, trying to cling to this moment before he chickened out and pretended like none of this happened. "I chased after people who didn't want me or didn't really love me. I've only ever wanted just one person, and I'm sorry it took me so many heartbreaks to realize that the kind of person I always wanted was you."

Hugo wasn't chickening out this time. By the grace of god, he was somehow making eye contact with me instead of shrinking away. He surveyed my face, his eyes deep and his breath quickening. I watched him waver, the nervous energy building between us, I felt my cheeks burn when his stare stopped on my lips.

I couldn't take it anymore. I'd been waiting all night for this exact moment.

"Are you going to kiss me or what?" I asked, hope swirling with adrenaline. I inched toward him, breathless and desperate to make this real.

"Ingrid," he chided, his seriousness vanishing in place of a bright grin. "If you were ever patient for once in your life, you would let me get up the nerve before I did."

"Hugo, if you wait one more second to do something you've wanted to do since middle school I'm going to—"

He chuckled to himself and caught me mid-sentence in a soft, close-mouthed kiss that tasted like buttered popcorn and Pepsi.

He did it. He actually did it.

And it was sweet. Not like my first kiss under the slide with Clayton—so fast, I thought I missed it—and not like Corey's wet, French kissing that left you feeling buzzed but empty. It was done around a smile. Warm, gentle. He tucked hair behind my ear as he did it and brushed his nose against mine as he pulled back.

"I know you've been kissed a lot before, so I'm sorry if that was bad," He said softly as he rested his forehead on mine.

Love radiated from me, and I cupped his face in my hands. "I should have known you'd be the only person who knows how to kiss me right."

His cheeks turned pink and he ducked his head away, suddenly bashful, but I chased after him and pressed another kiss to his lips. My fingers curled into his baby hairs and I pulled myself closer to him.

As a kid, I was convinced I would find my prince on this playground. Turns out, I was right.

Epilogue

I stand at the altar, bouquet in hand, smiling brightly. The church is perfumed with fresh flowers and draped in ribbons of beautiful wine-colored silks. My eyes water despite the smile splitting my face. It figures, I can hardly watch Say Yes to the Dress without sobbing. The officiant motions for the church to take their seats, and I look out into the pews for Hugo, who beams at me from the front row.

I look back to my mother, who stands across from Peter in a beautiful cropped white dress and birdcage veil. Peter is having a hard time keeping it together and looks as though he may burst into tears at any moment.

We've waited years for my mom and Peter to finally tie the knot. Apparently, they were waiting for my blessing—a blessing I didn't even know I was responsible for. So, when Mrs. Guerra finally asked them what they were waiting for and we got an explanation, I ordered that a wedding must happen immediately.

Enough was enough. They were clearly meant for each other, and they both deserved their happily ever after.

"You were my friend before you were anything else, and I regret not doing something sooner," my mom told Peter.

"I wasted so much time with people I didn't really like all because I didn't know I could have you—and when I finally got you, I couldn't believe how crazy I was never pursuing you. You're my best friend, my person, my knight in shining armor. You make this easy. I do. I do. I do."

I squeeze the bouquet in my hands tight as though it's Hugo I'm holding onto and I look for him in the front row. His eyes are welled up just like mine, and he nods to me as if to say I feel that way too.

Some people may say we're too young to know we'll end up together, but as I stand there, hands clasped around that bouquet, I can feel my engagement ring poking at my skin, and I know what happily ever after feels like. I do.

www.ingramcontent.com/pod-product-compliance
Lightning Source LLC
Chambersburg PA
CBHW070921190726
48292CB00004B/1054